BLUE

MAGGIE JOAN

For all the troubled souls out there. There is hope.

CHAPTER ONE

L ife was good. It had been a long time since I'd been able to even think such a thing. At fifteen years of age, I finally felt like I'd found somewhere I could call home, a *real* home.

Marsha, my foster mum, was everything you could ever dream of in a mum. Always smiling, she loved giving cuddles and kisses, and she baked, every day. From divine tasting bread to delicious cupcakes, I'd come to love nothing more than walking through the front door and having the sweet aroma of freshly baked goodies invade my senses.

Sitting on a deck chair in the back garden, shredding chunks of cheesy bread and scoffing it like I'd not eaten for a week, I sighed in contentment. A glass of homemade lemonade sat to my right, on a little white plastic table. Roger, Marsha's husband, my foster dad, had mowed the lawn this morning which meant the smell of freshly cut grass combined with the heat from the June sun made this moment absolutely perfect. I couldn't want for anything more right now.

My phone pinged with a text message, which I knew would be my friend Isabelle, or Izzy, demanding my time once again. Right now, though, I wanted nothing more than 'me' time in this idyllic moment.

Wearing my favourite red bikini, I nestled back into the chair and closed my eyes, touching my sunglasses to make sure they were in the right position. The sun heated my skin gently, my factor twenty sunscreen providing the perfect balance of protection and light bronzing.

I laid there long enough to slip into a cat nap, the true sign of complete happiness. I dreamed of walking through a daffodil field, my hands skimming the tops of the bright yellow flowers. The sun sat high in a bright cloudless sky. I found myself wearing a pretty white dress which billowed slightly as a cool breeze kissed my skin.

On the horizon, across the sea of yellow, something moved, something grey and big. It looked like an animal of some sort. As I walked towards it, I realised it was a horse, a beautiful grey horse. His ears were pricked, his head turned to watch me. His creamy white tail swished lazily from side to side, swatting the flies off his twitching skin.

Step by step, I approached him, he didn't move, or show any fear, he seemed as curious about me as I was him. Within a few feet of him, I held out my right hand for him to sniff, offering him a piece of reassurance I wouldn't hurt him. He reached out, blowing through his nose, his velvety soft muzzle millimetres from touching my fingers...

Ice cold water jolted me back to reality. I screamed from the shock, jumping up in an instant. Roaring laughter from my foster brother, Archie, had my blood boiling in seconds.

"Archie!" I yelled. "I'm going to kill you, you little s—"

"Blue!" Marsha shouted, stepping outdoors. "What have we said about your language?"

"But look!" I said, motioning to my soaking hair and body. "I was quite happy there and he had to come and ruin it, just like always."

Archie ran to Marsha and clasped his arms tightly around her soft middle in a proper 'save me' hug. The grin on his face made me want to strangle the little sod.

"He's eight years old, Blue," Marsha said, patting his dark head of hair like he was a good boy. "He just wants to play."

I took my sunglasses off and glared at the little prankster I hated so much. "Tell him to go and play with a bus or something then."

I plastered a sickly-sweet smile on my face and enjoyed Archie's look of horror. As always, to get the sympathy vote, he burst into tears.

"Blue, that was totally uncalled for and not very nice. Apologise to him please."

"When he apologises for doing this."

Marsha tilted her head to one side and sighed. That was the classic sign of me being in the wrong and here comes the lecture to prove it. "It was just some water, Blue. What you said was very hurtful and scary to a young boy. If he has nightmares, it will be your fault. You're the eldest one here so it's up to you to be the grown up in the situation and swallow your pride."

I used every ounce of willpower not to roll my eyes. "Yes, Marsha." I made eye contact with Archie again and said, "I'm sorry," in the least sarcastic voice I could muster.

He snuggled further into Marsha's side and stuck his tongue out at me. *I will get you, you little shit,* I thought to myself.

"See?" Marsha said. "Wasn't too hard, was it?"

I smiled at her and put my sunglasses back on. On the ground, two green water balloon skins lay burst open, the source of my untimely shower. I fought the urge to prove to her that he'd been in my room, again, but instead I silently promised that I would settle this sister to brother. After all the crap he'd pulled on me over the past seven months, revenge would be a sweet, sweet thing.

Sitting down on the now wet deck chair, I grabbed my phone and read my message.

Izzy: Want to head to the beach tonight?

I quirked an eyebrow up and grinned. That was Izzy's code for 'there's a party and we're going'. Scooping up the water balloon skins, I stood up, picked up the remainder of the cheesy bread, which was now a soggy mess, and headed indoors.

"You can thank Archie for that," I said to Marsha, giving her a smile as I plonked her ruined home baked bread down on the worktop.

She eyed the water dripping off it and

shrugged her shoulders. "I can always make some more, it's not a problem."

I tried my hardest not to let it irk me that that boy could do no wrong. Archie had been here before I arrived. Marsha had been fostering him since he was three and I think her and Roger had been thinking of adopting him. His story was a regular case of a hooked on drugs prostitute mum and an alcoholic abusive dad/pimp.

"I'm going to the beach with Izzy later," I said. "So I'll find my own tea."

"Have you done all your homework?"

I rolled my eyes. "Yes, not that there's much to do anyway. I've got like four days left before the summer holidays."

"You know the rules, Blue. Homework is homework."

"I know." I opened the cupboard above her head which was full of crisps, biscuits, and choco-late bars, and took a packet of unopened jammie dodgers.

"You'll spoil your tea," Marsha said.

"You mean my healthy fish and chips?" I replied, grinning.

"Get out of here," she said, laughing and swatting my bum with a tea towel. "Before Roger catches you."

I pecked her cheek lightly and ran upstairs to get changed. The cream long pile carpet felt so lush under my feet. It covered the entire upstairs of the house and I had been known to fall asleep on it more than once because of how soft and comfortable it was.

My bedroom sat at the front of the house. A big detached four-bedroom house, two master bedrooms were at the front, both with en suites, and two smaller bedrooms were at the back of the house, both still big enough for double beds and lots of furniture.

Archie viewed the modest sized bathroom as his considering the front bedrooms had en suites. What he didn't appreciate was that sometimes, people didn't want a shower and they wanted a nice long hot soak in a bubble bath. I should correct that, not people, me. Marsha and Roger could use 'his' bathroom as much as they pleased, but me, that was a different story.

When I'd first arrived here, just after New Year, I'd not had any form of bathing myself for a week. Imagine my delight when I walked into this beautifully clean, exquisitely decorated house, to not only discover they had a bath, but that it was clean, and I didn't have to share it with anyone. So excited, I'd almost cried and poured in half a bottle of *Radox 'Feel Restored' Lavender and Waterlily* bath soak. The bubbles were over a foot high and the water deliciously hot.

As the bath ran, Marsha showed me where the clean towels were kept in the spare back bedroom. They were gigantic bath sheets, pink for us girls and blue for the boys, and so soft and fluffy. I ran back to the bathroom, stripped off and jumped in, allowing a little tear to roll down my cheek in sheer joy.

And then I sat down. My moment of ecstasy became clouded when something gritty poked my bum and all along the backs of my legs. I dropped my hand in the water and felt along the bottom of the bath. To my sheer horror, the entire bathtub was covered in some sort of grainy material. I scraped some of it together and lifted it out of the water.

Salt.

I jumped out of the bath, wrapped myself up, and shouted for Marsha.

"What's up, sweetie?" she said, rushing to the bottom of the stairs.

"There's salt in the bath. Did you put that it in there for some reason?"

"No, poppet. I haven't been in the bathroom."

A creaking floorboard next to me turned my attention to the grinning eight-year-old child stood in his bedroom doorway. He shook a white plastic bottle labelled 'Table Salt' at me and stuck his tongue out.

My jaw dropped. "You little shit!"

I ran after him, Marsha ran up the stairs shouting my name, and Archie threw himself on the floor and hid under his bed. By the time Marsha came into the room, I was dragging him out, backwards, by an ankle. Archie was screaming like a cat trying to sing, and I was calling him all the names under the sun.

"Blue, let him go, now!"

I continued yanking on him as he refused to let go of the opposite side bed post.

"Mummy! Mummy!" he screamed.

"BLUE!" Marsha bellowed.

The booming voice coming from the sweet lady startled me into stopping. I stood up and backed away, my shoulders slumped and my head hanging low. This would be the part where I got a smack round the earhole or forced to go without food for a week.

I stood, trying not to shake, as Marsha coaxed Archie out from under the bed. She soothed him with lots of "It's ok, sweetpea," and "No one is mad at you," lines. The boy eventually emerged and threw himself around Marsha's waist.

"I was just trying to help, Mummy," Archie said, sniffling and looking up at Marsha with big puppy dog eyes. "I wanted to put bath salts in like when you do. I thought it would help."

Marsha hugged him to her side and kissed the top of his head. "That's very thoughtful of you, Archie, but not everyone likes bath salts, especially when they're not expecting them."

He nodded and sniffed again, then looked over at me and gave me the evil eye.

That was the beginning of my relationship with a miniature Satan.

CHAPTER TWO

S till formulating a plan of revenge for Archie, I walked along the street, sucking in a deep breath of fresh sea air. Despite how much that boy irritated me, living this close to the beach made up for it all. Where I currently lived, Polzeath in Cornwall, bested anywhere I'd lived to date.

Having never really stayed anywhere long enough to make friends, the fact I now had Izzy made everything so much brighter. I finally had a friend, one I trusted implicitly. She lived not far from me as her parents owned a holiday park in the village.

Izzy's route to the beach took her straight past the top of my road so I stopped and waited for her, as normal. I leaned back against the cobbled stone wall and looked up the hill, waiting eagerly for my best friend. Seconds later, her mop of fuzzy blonde hair appeared at the crest of the hill. Wearing her trademark skimpy shorts and a tight vest top, she had the body all teenage girls wanted—long legs, boobs that were actually boobs and not just fried eggs, and perfect skin.

"Helloooooo!" she yelled, waving her arms high up in the air.

I jumped up and mirrored her stance, shouting "Helllllloooooooooo," back.

She grinned and ran down to meet me. "Took you long enough to reply to me earlier, biatch."

Izzy loved her terms of endearment, even if some viewed them as not so endearing. Marsha didn't understand it at all.

"I was enjoying the sun and topping up my tan. Until Archie decided to throw water balloons on top of me."

She burst out laughing. "Oh, he's so adorable."

I raised an eyebrow and said flatly, "You live with him for a week and then tell me that."

"Happily. Get me away from cleaning caravans that people have been farting in for a week."

I giggled. "Week old farts, hmmm, I can just

taste it now." I stuck my tongue out and pretended to lick the air.

"Don't," she said, shoving me playfully. "Last week, someone had gone for a last-minute poo before they left and not bothered to check that it flushed." She put a hand to her mouth and started retching. "I can't even talk about it. It was too big to all go down the pan at once. Let's leave it at that."

I laughed at her and weighed up my options—do her job and have no Archie or live with Archie. It was a tough call. Either option involved dealing with a lot of unpleasantness.

"So, Aaron is going to be there tonight, and all of his crew." She nudged my side with her elbow. "That includes Regan."

I instantly blushed. "Regan isn't interested in me. He likes Poppy."

Izzy rolled her eyes. "Poppy is too much of a girly girl, all of that hair and her perfect gel nails, and don't even get me started on the cement mixer of make up on her face. Besides, she won't be coming tonight."

"Why?"

"She might get sand between her toes."

I giggled. "Some guys like all that though and I

13

think he's one of them. He wants a trophy and she's a perfect one."

"Yeah, a flat chested one," Izzy replied, snorting. "I've seen more curves on an ironing board."

I couldn't help but laugh and agree with her on that one. "When are you and Aaron making it official then?"

"Please," she said, ruffling her frizzy curls. "A girl always keeps her options open."

"Oh really," I said, raising my eyebrows at her. "And who are you keeping your options open for?"

She shrugged her shoulders and gave me a coy smile. "I don't know yet..."

I shook my head and smiled to myself. Izzy was the typical popular girl who had all the boys attention and an endless stream of girls who wanted to be her friend yet she still managed to feel insecure about something or someone, all the time. It baffled me.

As we approached the beach, the delicious smell of fish and chips cooking wafted over from the chip shop on my left. It sat on the corner of the road, the beach over the road from it.

"I'm so hungry," I said, fishing a ten-pound note from the back pocket of my jeans. "Want me to get a large so we can share?"

Izzy shook her head. "I'm on a milkshake only diet this week."

I grinned. Every week she had some new fad way of keeping in shape, or rather, staying slim. She hated exercise with a passion so deprived herself of calories instead, then once a week on a Friday, a.k.a Fat Friday, she'd binge on everything you could imagine and claim she was 'resetting her body' ready for the next week.

Skipping over the road and down to the beach, Izzy went ahead whilst I indulged in my tea. Freshly battered cod and new potato chips fresh out of the fryer, my stomach grumbled, and my mouth watered. I was bordering on drooling. I asked for them to be wrapped, rather than given to me in an open tray. It would stop people pinching my chips for one and it would also stop sand from getting in too.

That was a stringent thing about me—I didn't share food. I'd happily give someone the shirt off my back if they needed it, but food, no. That was all mine, unless I chose to share it, then you knew you'd made it into the 'special people' club, that to this date, only Izzy had gotten into.

Having to fight for my food from a young age had made me that way, plus a few incidents of spiteful foster kids who, jealous that I had food, would deliberately spoil mine so I'd go without too.

I pushed the bad memories away, this was not a time to be thinking about the past or why I was the way I was. I ambled out of the shop, food wrapped up nicely, and headed towards Izzy who I knew would be sat at our usual spot.

Eager to tuck into the delicious chips warming my hands, I picked up the pace and jogged across the sand towards a collection of rocks and washed up branches that sat at the far right of the beach. As I expected, Izzy had selected her usual favourite spot on top of the rocks. A flat surface had been smoothed into the rocks over the years, most likely from others who also loved the peace of this corner of the beach and the spectacular panoramic view it offered of the entire beach and the sea.

I threw my chips up onto the rocks next to Izzy so I could use both hands to clamber my way up. As I sat down next to her, I noticed she'd wrinkled her nose up in disgust.

"What's up with you?" I asked.

She shuffled away from me and pointed at my tea. "I can smell the grease on them, it's disgusting. It's actually making me feel sick."

I rolled my eyes and unwrapped them like a prize. "Oh, stop being such a princess."

"Look," she said, pointing at the grease marks on the paper. "You're putting that into your body. Doesn't that make you feel ill?"

I grinned and picked up a handful of chips. "I'd feel ill if I didn't eat." I put the chips into my mouth, one by one, until my cheeks were puffed out like a hamster. "Nom nom nom," I said, looking at her as I chewed.

She couldn't help but giggle. She stopped laughing for a moment, gasped, then laughed even harder.

"What?" I said, still struggling to finish my mouthful.

Izzy opened her mouth to talk but nothing came out except howls of laughter.

"Hey."

My entire body froze at the sound of that voice. I knew instantly why Izzy was laughing so much. What a biatch. My cheeks flaming with heat, I turned to see Aaron and Regan stood at the bottom of the rocks, grinning wildly.

My mouth too full to talk I put my hand up and waved. I felt like a right greedy cow. I resisted the urge to spit them all out and look gross but chewing quickly would make me look even worse. What a dilemma.

"Room up there for us?" Aaron asked, looking at a still giggling Izzy.

"If you can stand the stench of greasy chips," she replied, grinning at me.

"I think we can manage that," Regan said, giving me a cheeky wink.

My heart did a backflip. Izzy scooted to the furthest edge of the rocks, creating a gap in between us for the two boys. Aaron and his crew were the most popular boys at our school. Actually, most likely in our town. We'd nicknamed them One Direction because they were super-hot and always went everywhere together.

Aaron, with his spiky blonde hair, green eyes, and athletic body, was like the lead singer. All the girls gravitated towards him naturally, like he was a magnet and they were paper clips. Except me. I couldn't deny he was good looking but there was something about him that just felt off. I had yet to put my finger on it though.

Regan, wow, Regan. To me, he should have been more popular than Aaron. He played rugby so had a gorgeous built body with broad shoulders and muscled legs. His arms were full of toned muscles. Thanks to his Italian mother, he had the most delicious olive skin. Chocolate brown eyes I could stare into all day and thick glossy black hair with gentle curls I was dying to touch—Regan was the absolute personification of perfect.

They climbed up the rocks with ease, making it look like nothing more than running up a set of stairs. Aaron moved towards Izzy, slipping his arm around her shoulders. Her cheeks flushed pink and she giggled again.

Regan sat opposite me, our feet touching as they dangled over the rock edge, but my open fish and chips between us forcing us apart.

"How are you?" he asked, his eyes dancing with life.

My entire body erupted into goosebumps. I swallowed the last of my chips and said, "I'm good. How are you?"

"I was good," he said, emphasising the word 'was'. "But now I'm fantastic."

The serious edge to his words combined with his direct eye contact made me blush. Hot tingles surged all around my body and I couldn't do anything but look away.

"Why don't we switch places?" he said.

I frowned. "Why?"

"You're making me kinda nervous sat near the edge there."

I bit my lip to resist the 'aww' that wanted to escape. That was unbelievably sweet and so thoughtful. "What if you make me nervous sitting here?"

He curved his pink lips into a smile. "I'd rather have you nervous than falling off."

If he knew what I'd lived through, then he'd know that falling off fifteen-foot-high rocks would be like a walk in the park. However, I'd never been shown such a simple act of thoughtfulness, so I obliged. He offered me his hand to stand up, which I gladly took. His hands were almost double the size of mine and he towered over my petite five-five frame with his six-foot height. His skin was warm and surprisingly soft. As he guided me carefully around to where he'd been sitting, I couldn't help but look up at him and imagine for the briefest of moments that we were dancing.

"Are you going to prom?" he asked, not letting go of my hand until I'd sat back down.

"I hadn't really thought about it," I replied, shrugging my shoulders. "Are you?"

He nodded. "Kind of a tradition really. Like a

backwards initiation ceremony. You haven't offi-cially left school until you've attended prom."

I giggled. "Interesting take on it."

"I'm guessing you don't have a date yet then?"

My heart leapt into my mouth and I shook my head. Was he going to ask me? It would be like a lifetime of Christmases all at once if he did.

He broke out into a broad grin and winked. "I'm sure you'll have a queue of boys dying to ask you."

I spluttered with laughter. "You must be living in an alternate universe to me then."

"Not at all," he said. "But I do suggest you start dress shopping."

I couldn't help but grin like an idiot. Life wasn't good. It was bloody marvellous.

CHAPTER THREE

Needless to say, after Regan's appearance, my fish and chips soon went cold. My appetite completely vanished because I was happily full of spending some quality time with Regan. As twilight fell, the rest of Aaron's crew turned up—Max, Eddie, Barney, Michael, and Jake —all with booze and radios.

Max and Eddie concentrated on starting a fire, having hauled a couple of bags of logs along with them. The other three set up the music and cracked open a can of beer each.

"We're going down there to grab a beer," Izzy said. "You coming?"

I wasn't fond of alcohol. Ok, that was a slight understatement. I absolutely detested the stuff but that was my problem to deal with. I wouldn't expect others to not enjoy it because of my aberration to it.

"I'm good," I said, smiling up at her.

She rolled her eyes but said nothing more. She didn't know why I hated alcohol but had enough sense to realise it related to my past.

"Are you cold?" Regan asked, drawing my attention back to him.

I shook my head. "I've always been a hot kind of person."

"I can see that," he said, a mischievous glint in his eye.

I giggled and looked away. I'd never been the focus of anyone's attention, not like this, let alone paid compliments. To say I didn't know how to react would be putting it very lightly.

"I was going to suggest moving closer to the fire if you were cold," he said, inching his way towards me.

My heart tripled in speed. The spicy tones of his aftershave drifted towards me, making me want to suck in a deep breath to take in all that I could.

"I'm good, thank you. I kinda like it up here. It's quiet and peaceful but still close enough to the party."

He nodded. "It's like we're in a dark corner of the school hall at a disco or something."

I agreed with him. We had perfect low lighting, were sat close enough to the party, but were far enough away to enjoy things with just us two. Shadows from the flames danced around at our feet on the rock faces and remembering that people can't see from light into dark, we genuinely did have the best seats in the house. We could see them but not vice versa.

We indulged in some general chit chat about TV shows and films we liked, all the while gazing out from our vantage point over the scene in front of us. At least a dozen more people had joined since twilight blended into darkness.

Regan moved closer to me, our legs now touching. "Is this ok?" he whispered.

My pulse now racing, I nodded. In true me style, I had to say something to sabotage it. "What about Poppy?"

"It's complicated," he said, sighing.

I closed my eyes and sighed. I liked this guy, a lot, but that didn't mean I would excuse him potentially cheating. "I don't believe in two-timing, Regan. It's not fair."

"No, no, no," he said. "It's nothing like that.

She really likes me but I'm not into her like that. Aaron likes the idea of me and her though because they're cousins and he wants someone who will look after her."

I raised my eyebrows. "They're cousins?"

He nodded. "Not many people know that. Her dad and his mum are brother and sister. Her home life is pretty rubbish, she doesn't have it easy and I kind of feel like I have to be nice to her because Aaron is my best friend, but she takes anything from me as me liking her like that and I don't. She's totally not my type."

"Have you told her you don't like her like that?"

"Yep. She doesn't believe me though. Thinks I'm running from my feelings for her."

I laughed. "Isn't that called being delusional?"

"I think it's just called being Poppy."

We both laughed. Hearing him explain the situation eased my worries to pretty much nothing. It now made sense why he walked her home and carried her schoolbooks for her. He was being a dutiful friend to Aaron in helping to look after his family.

"I'm guessing you're taking her to prom then?"

"I haven't asked her and I have no intentions of

doing so. I'm trying to bribe Eddie into asking her but it's not working so far. He's a tough one to please."

"Why Eddie?"

"They were childhood sweethearts like way back in primary school. Eddie hasn't really had an interest in anyone, so I thought they'd be a good fit."

"That would be quite sweet. They start school being sweethearts and maybe end school being sweethearts."

Regan nodded. "Exactly what I thought too. Unfortunately, Eddie doesn't seem to think so."

"Maybe he's seeing someone you don't know about? Someone who isn't from our school?"

He looked at me, his eyes gleaming. "Of course. I hadn't even thought about that. You are such a little genius."

"I wouldn't go that far."

He lifted a hand and brushed a stray hair back from my face. "I definitely would."

My entire body leapt into overdrive. The way he was staring at me, the closeness between us, the atmosphere we were in, I knew he was going to kiss me. My heart jumped up and down with joy whilst my head could only think of one word—yes!

He closed the gap between us, cupping my cheek with one hand. As he was about to kiss me, I heard a, "Hey, Regan."

I turned my head to see Poppy and her followers stood at the bottom of the rocks, staring up at us.

"Hey, Poppy," Regan said, moving away from me.

The instant he moved away from me, an over-whelming urge of disappointment washed over me. Not because we'd been about to kiss and she'd interrupted it, but because he'd intentionally made space between us. It was as if he were trying to hide the fact something might have been about to happen.

Maybe this whole situation with her was more complicated than what he made it out to be. Was the idea of me and him just a dream as oppose to a potential reality?

"Can we talk?" Poppy asked him.

"Sure," he said. As he turned to stand up and climb back down, he whispered, "Stay here. I'll be back."

A swell of excitement rose inside me and I bit my lip to contain the grin that wanted to break out.

Maybe my dream could be a reality. Only time would tell.

I sat on the rocks for an hour waiting for Regan to return. With each passing moment, my hope evaporated into a depressing reality. As I realised he likely wasn't going to return, I bit back my frustration and climbed down from the rocks.

Making my way over to the fire, I could see Izzy with her tongue down Aaron's throat. I grinned and rolled my eyes. So much for keeping her options open. I looked around for Regan, squinting my eyes into the darkness as much as I could in the hopes of catching sight of him, but my efforts were fruitless. When I realised that Poppy planned on keeping him for the rest of the night, I slinked away back home, biting back disappointment.

CHAPTER FOUR

"Hey," Izzy said, bounding up to me at school with a huge smile on her face. "Where did you disappear to last night?"

I closed my locker and forced a smile back. "I got bored so I went home."

"From what I hear, you were far from bored," she said, nudging my shoulder and winking.

"What do you mean?"

"Apparently Poppy saw you and Regan kissing."

I rolled my eyes and sighed. "No, we didn't kiss. We were about to kiss and then she magically appeared."

Izzy laughed. "It's like she has a sixth sense when it comes to Regan."

"No kidding. He went off to talk to her and said he'd come back but didn't." I shrugged my shoulders. "I guess that's that."

"I'm going into town at lunch with Aaron. Wanna come?"

I shook my head. "No, thanks."

"Why not?"

"Just don't feel like it."

"Awww, is someone lovesick?"

"No," I replied, my cheeks flaring with heat. "I just can't be bothered."

"Ok, well if you change your mind, text me."

She turned and flounced off to her next class just as the bell rang. I hugged my books closer to my chest and headed towards biology.

"What's this?" I asked, frowning.

"It's a letter," Izzy said, pushing it at me. "From Regan."

I frowned. "Why didn't he just text me?"

"I don't know," she replied, shrugging her shoulders. "Don't shoot the messenger. Aaron gave it to me at lunch and asked me to pass it on to you."

I ambled outside and sat down on the neatly

trimmed grass, leaning back against one of the old oak trees to read this mysterious letter.

As soon as I opened it, I recognised Regan's handwriting. Flowing letters written with a fountain pen, almost an italic tilt to it, his handwriting really was an art all on its own. His mother loved calligraphy, so he'd told me once, and I guessed that's where his beautiful script had come from.

Hey Blue, I'm so sorry about last night at the beach. I meant to come back, and every part of me wanted to, but something came up and I had to go. I've lost my phone, hence writing to you. I didn't want you to think I don't care because I really do. I like you a lot and I know you like me too. Do you think we could maybe meet at Arlene's after school? I'd love to spend some time with you again, just me and you. I'll be waiting for you at 4pm, sharp. Regan x

I bit my lip to curb my excitement. Everything made sense now. I hadn't seen him at school today so guessed he must have had a family emergency or something last night. Arlene's was my favourite place in town, a beautiful quaint corner café that served the best toasted sandwiches and freshly squeezed orange juice. My stomach grumbled just at the thought of it.

Was this a date? I forced myself to contain a squeal of joy. It must be, right? He'd asked me to meet him somewhere, outside of school, somewhere that served food and drink. This was a date.

The rest of school dragged like hell. Each minute that ticked away felt like an eternity. Finally, when the bell rang at the end of the day at three-thirty, I picked up my stuff, ran to my locker, and then dashed to the bathroom to make sure I looked presentable enough. I finger combed my hair and ruffled it up a little then put some of my Burts Bees tinted lip balm on. The soft pink tones it left behind looked fantastic against my make up free face.

Like a kid at Christmas, I dodged my way through the throng of kids trying to make their way outside to the buses and headed for town. I checked my watch—twenty minutes to go. I'd be there in about ten minutes. My stomach did backflips and my heart pounded against my ribs, jumping up into my throat every so often.

As I approached Arlene's, I scanned over the tables and chairs outside, but he wasn't there. Reminding myself this was a proper date, I realised he would most likely be waiting inside. I resisted the urge to skip or run and tried to act as cool and casual as possible as I wandered inside the cosy little building.

I stood in the doorway, looking around in case he was here early. The booths that lined the right hand wall were all taken except for an empty one at the back. The tables to the left were mostly taken but no sign of Regan. Heading for the booth at the back so we had some privacy, I chewed on my tongue to distract my mind from the anticipation of seeing Regan walk through the door.

Despite reading the menu to try and keep myself busy, I found my eyes glued to the door and the outside windows, eager to catch a glimpse of him. I checked the time on my phone—two minutes to four. My stomach fluttered and my mind flooded with images of his gorgeous chocolate eyes lighting up when he saw me.

"Would you like anything to drink?"

A tall blonde waitress stood at the side of the table, pad and pen in hand ready for my order. "Orange juice please. Actually, make that two. I'm waiting for someone."

She nodded as she scribbled it down on her pad and headed back to the kitchen. I knew from my chat with Regan last night that he loved fresh smooth orange juice, no bits. Just the way I liked it too. My heart was in my mouth as I caught sight of every dark haired person that walked past the windows. None of them Regan, yet.

I checked my phone again—one minute past four. I frowned and smiled. He'd said four p.m. sharp. This wasn't so sharp. But then again, people's watches and phones could easily be out of sync by up to five minutes.

The waitress returned then with our glasses of juice. "Would you like to order food now or wait until your friend gets here?"

"I'll wait until he's here if you don't mind please?"

She nodded and walked away.

I took a sip of my juice and revelled in the cold fresh drink on a warm summers day. With my nerves on the verge of boiling over, I found myself scrolling through Facebook just to keep my attention on something. By the time the clock ticked over to ten past four, my nerves were turning into dread. Was he actually coming? I thought about ringing him but then remembered he'd lost his phone.

The waitress came back over then and asked if I wanted to order something. I sighed and asked to wait another five minutes. Tapping her pen against her pad, she disappeared once more.

I gave up with Facebook and leaned back against the white booth wall, staring at the door in hope. When the clock ticked over to twenty past four, I began to face reality that he wasn't coming. Maybe something had happened that meant he couldn't make it. Without a phone though, he couldn't let me know otherwise.

When the waitress came back at half past, I sighed in defeat and ordered a cheese, tomato, and onion toastie with some sweet potato fries on the side. It made sense to eat here anyway as Archie had demanded gammon for tea which he knew I hated but of course, Marsha always indulged him.

By five o clock, I admitted defeat and after paying the bill, left. A strange mix of emotions tumbled around inside me. Disappointment, stupidity, confusion—they all churned together leaving behind a rising wave of bitterness that I swear I could literally taste on my tongue.

It didn't take me too long to walk home and I arrived just as Marsha served up tea.

"Hey, sweetie," she said, giving me a warm smile. "Have you had a good day?"

"Not bad, thank you. I've already eaten so I'm going to head up for a shower."

Marsha's face creased into worry. "Are you ok?"

I nodded. "Just been a long day."

"Do you want to talk about it?"

I smiled. "Maybe later."

Marsha nodded. "I'm always here for you, Blue, remember that. Can you send Archie down please?"

I nodded and headed upstairs, wondering how much I'd get shouted at if I sent Archie down the stairs with my foot up his ass.

"Archie, it's teatime," I said, throwing my bag onto my bed and walking into the bathroom.

As I looked at the long, deep bath, I changed my mind on the shower and started to run a bath. Hearing nothing from my delightful foster brother, I went into his room to see him on his laptop, staring at me over the top of it.

He pointed at me, shut the lid, and laughed.

I rolled my eyes and folded my arms over my chest. "Your tea is ready."

"Hahahahahaha, you're so stupid, Blue." He got up and skipped across his room. "Blue is stupid, waiting for Cupid."

He continued his ridiculous little chant all the way down the stairs. I ignored his ridiculous teasing and shut myself away in the bathroom before I did something I might regret. I sank into the hot water and piles of bubbles, letting the rising water envelope my days stress and wash it away.

I'd left my phone in my bag which meant my bath was nothing but total freedom and peace. As I usually did in the bath, my eyes started drooping and I gave in to a power nap. Typically, when I woke up, my skin had wrinkled to resemble something like a prune, but I didn't care. I felt absolutely revitalised, happy, and like I could take on the world.

After washing myself down, I wrapped myself up in a big pink bath sheet and headed for my room. I threw my bag on the floor, decided to ignore my phone for the night, and climbed into bed. My alarm clock told me I'd been in the bath for over an hour with it now being just after seven p.m. I flicked on my TV and settled down for the night. I felt good again. Life really was good.

CHAPTER FIVE

The next morning was nothing unusual. I woke up late, ran around like a headless chicken, grabbed a piece of toast on my way out of the door and yelled my goodbyes. It was made even better by the fact I hadn't seen the annoying little shit either.

I power walked to school, munching on my jam covered toast, and sighed in contentment. As I rounded the corner of the street where school was, I heard the bell ring. I swore at myself and ran for the gates, stuffing the last of my breakfast in my mouth.

Running through the corridors, I made it to my classroom just as the last kids were filing in. I breathed a sigh of relief and followed them in, trying my best to look cool and nonchalant. As I always did, I scanned the room for my seat—next to the window, third from the back.

Some of the others started giggling and snickering, whispering to one another as I walked in. I frowned and thought nothing of it. I'd faced countless scenarios like this and had come to terms with the fact that I would always be an outsider looking in. The cool kids, the 'in' crowd would never accept someone like me but that was ok. If they needed to laugh and make snide comments to one another then they really needed a stark reality check if that was all they had to worry about in life.

Mrs Mace strode through the door, her short but bulky frame commanding attention as always. With her black hair cut just above her ears and her brown eyes piercing through anyone she looked at, Mrs Mace was a formidable person, let alone a teacher. She stood for no nonsense whatsoever. Most kids were terrified of her. There were rumours she'd been in the military which wouldn't surprise me given her direct approach and need for things to be 'just so'.

As the door slammed shut behind her, most of the giggling stopped, but I could still hear some whispers and sniggering from behind me.

Mrs Mace narrowed her eyes straight down the classroom. "Georgie, Emily, perhaps you'd like to come to the front of the class and tell the rest of us what is so amusing this morning."

"No, Miss," said Georgie, her squeaky voice sending shivers right through me.

Mrs Mace gave her a lazy but rather sadistic smile. "It wasn't a question."

Several seconds later, two chairs scraped back across the floor and Georgie and Emily shuffled their way to the front of the classroom. Emily looked petrified, her blue eyes pinned wide open with fear like a rabbit caught in headlights. Her long blonde hair hung down around her and she started fiddling with it. Georgie, her brown hair piled up high on top of her head, crossed her arms over her chest and actually dared to smirk at Mrs Mace.

I bit my lip to stifle a giggle. Boy would she be in for it now.

Mrs Mace gestured with her arm towards the room. "Please, go ahead," she said. "Enlighten us all so we can be entertained along with you. After all, education is just a big joke."

The room fell silent, the atmosphere so tense it felt like I could reach out and touch it. I think every single one of us held our breath, waiting for Georgie's next move. She was one of the popular cool kids, a leader of the 'in' crowd. What she did next would reflect on her reputation at school.

"Nothing, Miss," Georgie said, clearing her throat. "We were just talking about something we saw on TV last night."

"Oh, well, do tell, Georgie, please."

Georgie's pale cheeks flushed bright red. "Oh it was nothing, really, just a funny scene from a show we both watch."

Mrs Mace nodded her head slowly. "Considering you were rude enough to ignore my presence in the room then it must have been more than funny. Please share it with us."

I sucked in a deep breath. I wouldn't swap places with Georgie right now even for a winning lottery ticket.

"You kinda have to watch the show to get it," she said, unfolding her arms and wringing her hands together. "One of those things where you have to be there."

"What about you, Emily?" Mrs Mace said, looking around Georgie to the quieter girl. "Perhaps you'd like to share this hilarious scene with us?"

Emily looked down at shook her head. "No, Miss. I'm sorry, Miss."

"Both of you would do well to remember that manners cost nothing and get you everything. Now, go and sit down and if I hear one more peep from either of you, you're in detention at lunch."

"Yes, Miss. Thank you, Miss," Emily said, scurrying back to her seat with a tomato-coloured face.

Georgie said nothing as she ambled back to her desk, head held high and her shoulders squared back. She looked at me and grinned. Not a friendly grin, a proper wide toothy grin that said the joke was on me. My heart lurched and straight away I wondered if I'd got crumbs or jam from my toast around my mouth. As she sat down behind me, I patted around my mouth but couldn't feel any sticky residue or leftover food. I frowned and shrugged it off.

As the day wore on, I became more and more aware of people whispering and giggling wherever I went. By lunchtime, I knew it wasn't my imagination or the fact I'd left my breakfast around my mouth.

I collared Izzy in the dining hall. "Why is everyone looking at me and laughing today?"

She looked away, catching my eyes for the

briefest of seconds before she replied, "They're not. You're just being paranoid."

I looked around me as I queued up for dinner and spotted another group of giggling girls just the other side of the till. "Look," I said, inclining my head in their direction. "They're looking at me and laughing."

"No, they're not," she said, taking a plate from the side and eyeing up the hot food.

I sighed and closed my mouth. I picked up a slice of pizza and two pieces of garlic bread. Comfort food was more than needed today. Still unable to shake the feeling of something being off, I dared to take another look around the room. Sure enough, hundreds of eyes were on me, every last one shining with delight at something.

As I reached the counter to pay, a tall geeky boy from the year below me approached the till, his thin lips twisted up into a quirky smile and his green eyes glistening with pleasure.

"I'll get this," he said, talking to the dinner lady.

I froze, unsure what to do or say. I'd never so much as spoken to this boy let alone done anything else that warranted him buying my dinner.

46

"You don't have to do that," I said, smiling at him.

"Sure, I do. You helped me win a lot of money," he said, handing over a five-pound note to the dinner lady. "It's the least I can do."

I frowned, my mind racing with possibilities as to what he could mean. "I'm sorry, what? I don't even know your name."

"Tom," he said, taking his change back from the dinner lady. "Tom Bradford. Thanks again."

The dinner lady smiled at me and waved me through past her. I navigated my way through the crowded hall and found a spot in the far corner, nearest the door. A group of younger lads laughed as I sat down. What the hell was going on?

I caught Izzy's eye as she surveyed where to sit and waved her over. She smiled at me but went to sit with Aaron, Jake, Barney, and Max. Ouch. That was a kick in the teeth. Feeling like an animal being stared at in a zoo, I wolfed down my food and slinked out of the dining hall. I hated being in my form room at lunch but today I wanted the safety of it.

As I approached the door, I heard roaring laughter coming from inside. I walked in, my eyes automatically drawn to the group of girls in the corner.

"I can't believe she actually bought this crap. How desperate can someone be?" one of the girls said. Her voice sounded a lot like Poppy's.

The girls all laughed. I froze. Instantly, I knew this was about me. Nausea swarmed me and raging heat burned through my face. What was going on?

"Let's have a look again," someone else said. "You really did copy his handwriting well. It's genius."

"I can't believe Tom Bradford of all people won the bet," said another, snorting in disdain. "The pot was well over two hundred quid. Jammy sod."

"I'm amazed she lasted over an hour," said another. "Although technically, her eating shouldn't count."

"You're just sore because you lost out by two minutes," said the Poppy sounding voice.

I didn't know what to think, do, or even say. I just stood there like a complete dork, staring at them all. They'd been betting on me? I started shaking from a mixture of fear and anger. Water glazed over my eyes turning them all into hazy shapes.

"Guys," one of the girls said, looking at me.

The group parted to reveal Poppy sat in my seat, a triumphant grin all over her face. "Hey," she said, standing up. "Did you enjoy your food last night?"

"What is this? What's going on?" I asked, my voice shaking.

Poppy snatched the letter back from one of her cronies and held it up. "Did you honestly think he'd write *you* a letter? Especially a letter like this?"

I opened my mouth but I had no words.

"You actually thought he'd be interested in *you* over *me*?" She laughed, her group of followers laughing with her. "Take this as me letting you down gently, on behalf of Regan. If you so much as even look at him again, I'll cause you a world of pain you never knew existed."

An overwhelming urge to run took over my body. My mind was blank, numb, and I couldn't act on anything other than pure instinct. I fled, running as if the devil himself were chasing me. I didn't even stop for my bag—all that mattered was getting away from this negative situation as quickly as possible. Without thinking, I ran for the beach, for my favourite place on top of those rocks, away from people.

Laughter chased me all the way out of school

fuelling me even more. By the time I reached my place of solace, my legs were on fire and my lungs burning for air. My cheeks were wet with streaks of tears. Despite my trembling, I somehow managed to climb the rocks and collapse on top of them.

CHAPTER SIX

Marsha didn't understand my dilemma. To be honest, I hadn't expected her to but that didn't mean I couldn't hope.

"Everything will be just fine," she said, sitting at the end of my bed that night. "It'll be yesterday's news by tomorrow."

I shook my head. "You don't understand, Marsha. The entire school was betting on me and how long I'd sit there waiting like some sad loser. The video went viral. Even he saw it!" I said, pointing towards Archie's room.

Marsha giggled. "It went what?"

"Viral."

"Not bacterial then?"

I rolled my eyes and resisted the urge to scream. "This isn't funny. This is my life!"

Still chuckling, Marsha patted my legs before she stood up to leave. "It will all be forgotten by next week at the latest. You can weather this storm, Blue. You're a tough cookie."

My heart sank and my mind wandered back to the children's home I'd had the misfortune of being in for a few months when I was eight. I'd been missing for a few weeks after running away from a particularly nasty foster family. The father was nothing short of a male chauvinist pig and viewed any female, regardless of age, as a servant to him and his needs. *Any* needs.

When the cops picked me up one November night, sleeping on a park bench, I thought I'd been rescued. Freezing cold, starving hungry, and unbathed for weeks, I literally was something from a Charles Dickens novel. I was very mistrusting of men and was almost hysterical when the male copper approached me. Luckily, he had a female colleague with him who calmed me down or God knows what I might have done.

They took me back to the station, wrapped me up in blankets, and fed me some delicious tomato soup. I'd never been more grateful for such a simple meal in all my life. Even now, it was my comfort food, something that reminded me of that lovely police lady, Emma, and the fact that good in this world did exist.

Middle aged, blonde, and petite, Emma immediately came across as someone quiet and calm, someone not to fear. She sat with me all night, even after her shift ended, until the authorities came to pick me up the next morning. I'd clung onto her kindness and reassuring energy like a gecko.

The next morning, a tall, stern looking man walked in and introduced himself as Tim. He explained that he ran a children's home, and I would be staying there with him and lots of other children until they could find a suitable foster family for me. I remember shaking my head and crying into my blanket, refusing to be anywhere near a man.

"I told you she needed a woman," Emma whispered to him.

He shrugged his shoulders. "My colleague, Sandy, is away today on other business. I'm the only option."

Emma sighed. "Then I'll come with you."

"That's really not necessary."

"Not to you, no, but it is for her."

Just like that, darling Emma accompanied me to the children's home. She drove me in her own car, following the unsympathetic Tim. We wound around some twisty backroads in the beautiful countryside of Taunton. When a huge red bricked house appeared on the horizon, splayed out over perfectly landscaped gardens, I started to get excited.

"Is that where we're going?" I asked Emma.

"It sure is, honey. You're going to have so much fun there. There's so many other children, just like you, who need friends and someone to play with. You'll have your own room and as much ice cream as you can dream of."

I grinned like a Cheshire cat and finally felt some hope as we pulled into the huge sweeping driveway. I'd never felt such amazing hope rising inside me. As Tim pulled up outside, some older kids came outside, staring at me like I was an alien, but some of them were girls and that made me feel a hundred times easier. I wasn't alone here and that was a great feeling.

"You look after yourself," Emma said, helping me out of the car. "You're a tough little cookie."

I nodded and willed myself not to cry. Something about Emma made me want to stay with her forever. "Thank you."

"You're very welcome. Now, go and have a good life."

Tim instructed one of the older girls to come and get me. A chubby brunette with a big nose and glasses came down the steps with a hand outstretched. "Come on, sweetie, let's get you settled."

Like a meek little lamb, I took her hand and followed her inside, promises of ice cream and a good life dazzling my mind like stars in my eyes. I heard a car pulling away outside, the gravel crunching beneath the tyres. I turned my head to look behind me, to see if I could catch a final glimpse of Emma, the lovely lady who gave me soup, blankets, and a ray of hope.

"Don't look back," the chubby girl said. "We all look forward now. Looking back does no good."

Her cryptic message confused me, and I couldn't help but frown as I tried to work it out. She led me into a huge living room where a giant flatscreen TV blared out music videos to several girls who were watching it and copying the dance moves of the pop star on the screen.

At the far end, a long dark wooden dining table

gleamed under the spotlights in the ceiling. The umpteen chairs were empty except for one.

An older lady with greying blonde hair looked up from a pile of paperwork, her blue eyes dulled over, and her cheeks flushed pink.

"Hey there, cutie," she said, smiling a smile that didn't quite reach her eyes. "And who might you be?"

"Blue," I said, tugging at my blanket with my free hand.

"That's a lovely name you have there. Nice to meet you, Blue. I'm Sandy."

My eyes widened and fear flooded me in an instant. My survival instinct kicked in and I screamed, "Emma!"

I woke up, covered in sweat, heaving for breath. I quickly surveyed my surroundings and breathed a sigh of relief when I found myself in my usual bed, in Marsha's house. Throwing the bed covers back, I kicked my legs over the side of the bed and took a few minutes to return to reality.

My alarm clock told me it was eleven-thirty p.m. That meant in less than twelve hours, I'd be in school. My stomach churned with dread and humiliation at the thought of facing everyone and being laughed at all over again. When I had no idea why people were laughing at me, it was ok, but the fact I now knew why changed everything. I was nothing but the sad outsider, the poor foster kid who was nothing but a real-life toy for other people's amusement.

Thoughts of Tim tried to force themselves to the front of my mind, but I pushed them away. Then it struck me. Marsha's jovial light-hearted reaction to my plight was no different to how Sandy had been.

"Oh my god," I whispered, as the penny dropped.

I scrambled to my feet, self-preservation kicking in once more. I had to get out of here. Marsha wasn't going to take me any more seriously than what Sandy had done all those years ago. I knew this whole thing was too good to be true; finally having the perfect life with the perfect foster parents—it didn't exist, it was all a dream, a stupid ridiculous dream.

"How could I have been so stupid?" I muttered to myself as I quietly picked my way around my room. "If something is too good to be true then it is, stupid. Stupid, stupid, stupid."

I needed to carry light. I'd learned that over the years. Big backpacks drew attention from well-trained eyes to know when someone wasn't staying at home. Carrying bare essentials in a regular shoulder bag made you look like you were going about your day-to-day life—providing you looked clean and presentable.

Over my time as a runaway, I'd developed an emergency escape kit. I didn't keep it all together stashed in a neat little bag because that would rouse suspicion from any nosey foster parents or social workers who decided to investigate my personal space whilst I wasn't there. However, the items spread around the room at various points seemed like nothing out of the ordinary. I reached for the regular items—chewing gum, hairbrush, purse with money in it, mini torch, lip balm, baby wipes, soap, and tampons.

Tampons used to be a tricky area. Being feminine hygiene, they normally belong in the bathroom. However, Archie had been useful for one thing and that was allowing me to have them in my room. Not long after I came to live with Marsha and Roger, I had a period. I went to my tampon box and opened it to find the entire box filled with tampons that had been dipped in red paint.

Roger found it amusing and Marsha put it

down to him being a playful little boy who didn't understand about things like that.

"He's coloured them red, Marsha," I yelled. "He damn well knows."

"He's just a child. Don't worry, I'll get you some more."

And that was it—Archie's telling off over. However, I had been allowed to keep them in my room, well hidden from his grubby little hands ever since. It meant I had one less room to go to before I left which also meant less chance of waking someone up.

I had a small silver box which I kept padlocked and underneath my bed, right back against the far wall in the corner. Marsha had demanded to know its contents when I first arrived, but I told her it was personal and sentimental at which point she left it alone.

Archie, however, viewed it as a challenge. I found him one day, about three weeks after I'd moved in, trying to prise it open with a screwdriver. Marsha had gone food shopping and Roger had been outside in the garden which meant the little shit was at my mercy.

"What the hell do you think you're doing?" I

yelled, running into my room and snatching the box away from him.

"I want to know what's in there," he said, narrowing his eyes at me.

"Nothing that concerns you."

"I don't care. I want to know."

"I want never gets."

He stuck his tongue out at me. "Well I do so ner."

I grabbed the screwdriver from his hand, picked him up by his hair and tilted his head back. Pointing the tip of the screwdriver millimetres from his eye, I gave him the most sadistic grin I could and said, "Is it worth your eyeball?"

He started shaking and crying. "No."

"Good," I said, moving the screwdriver away from him. "Because if I catch you anywhere near that ever again, I'll dig your eyes out with this screwdriver. Got it?"

He squealed and nodded.

When the overwhelming stench of urine hit my nose, I looked down to see he'd peed himself. I rolled my eyes and let him go. "And if you piss yourself in my room again, I'll cut your willy off with this as well."

He turned and ran into his bedroom, crying his

eyes out. I knew boys like him; they were two a penny. Mortified by the fact he'd weed himself, he wouldn't say a single word about our chat.

To this day, he hadn't. And he also hadn't gone anywhere near my box again. I knew that for sure because I'd placed things around it in a specific way that would tell me otherwise.

There was nothing sentimental in the box, but it was personal. After years of fighting for food or going hungry in various foster homes, as soon as I'd been able to earn money, I'd saved every penny up to buy myself a secret stash of food so I'd never go hungry again.

But this wasn't your regular run of the mill crisps and crackers. This was proper hardcore stuff survivalists and preppers bought. Dry biscuits and protein bars packed with calories, emergency ration food, freeze dried fruit. I even had a box of storm matches in there that I'd gotten as a free gift, and a bottle of iodine for purifying water. I was all set.

Except of course, my crème de la crème—my Scrubba bag. Being on the run meant looking half decent and you couldn't do that with dirty clothes you'd been wearing for three weeks. This little beauty however meant I could wash my clothes wherever there was water.

I threw it all into my corduroy shoulder bag, grabbed my blanket, the one I still treasured from Emma, and headed down the stairs. Time to survive yet again.

CHAPTER SEVEN

I crept outside, closing the door behind me. Being June, the night air warmed my skin instead of chilling it. My habit of running away had seemed to always take place in the winter months before now. Running away seemed like a coward's way out to most people but it's far from that. It boils down to the basic fight or flight instinct.

Facing humiliation by three hundred hormone ridden teenagers would do more damage to me mentally than any shrink could ever undo. Marsha didn't understand it, but that was ok because not many people could understand the things that teenagers have to live through, especially with a history like mine. With Marsha unable to guide me or help me, I had to resort to what I knew best—fleeing the danger before it struck.

I headed for the coast, intending to walk the coastal path north. I knew there was a youth hostel in Tintagel. If I could make the four hour walk during the small hours then I'd be there already by the time Marsha and Roger woke up and realised I'd gone. I had nearly five hundred pounds in cash on me which I'd earned from various menial jobs and the odd cigarette carton selling here and there.

A full moon and a clear sky highlighted my path perfectly. As I hurried down towards the beach, I took a minute to appreciate the beautiful village in all its glory. It really was the epitome of a sleepy coastal village with scenic views and locals who had lived here all their lives for several generations. The only shame was the younger generation growing up, void of manners and respect, and poisoning it for the future. Without the tourism every summer, small places with local run businesses wouldn't survive.

I picked up the coastal path and scanned the ground ahead of me for potential potholes, dips, dead animals, or anything else I could trip up over. Injuries were easily sustained when not being careful and just blind running to get away from something. The survival instinct was a powerful force, an in-built natural danger detector. To consciously override it and think rationally took a lot of practice.

As I picked my way over the uneven, well-worn, dusty path, I found myself musing over my life. Nearly ten years had gone by since my life unravelled around me like a tragic Shakespearean play. My mother, Nancy, hadn't been much of a mum, to what I recall.

Most of my early childhood memories involved playing on my own in a dark room with broken toys —one legged dolls, or teddies with no stuffing, or crayons that couldn't be sharpened anymore or they'd disintegrate into nothing. My clothes had always been either too big or too small and I'd always worn them for at least two days. Kids at school had teased me, pulling on my unbrushed hair, or holding their noses and telling me I smelled, or even spoiling the single bread and butter sandwich I had every day for lunch just for the hell of it.

I loved my mum though. Her big brown eyes and pink rosy cheeks were always accompanied by a warm smile at the end of every day—a smile that took the chill right out of my soul. We would sit and eat together, sometimes Mum not even eating because she couldn't afford to feed both of us, but I'd insist on sharing my food with her which always filled her Bambi eyes with tears.

Her boyfriend, my dad, liked to pretend I didn't even exist. I'd learned very quickly to get out of his way and stay out of his way because he would literally walk right through me. I'd suffered a broken wrist at age four because I didn't get out of his way quick enough and he knocked me flying into a wall.

I still remember the searing pain that made me howl like anything. Mum had tried her best to soothe me, telling me she would fix it, it would all be ok, but we couldn't go to the doctor because then he'd take me away from her. That made me cry even harder. I loved my mummy.

Two weeks off school spent with a heavily bandaged wrist and what I now know to have been a splint, I was thrown back into normal everyday life with a wrist support to help me through the remainder of my healing. Mum had told the teachers I'd fallen off a pony in my first riding lesson. They seemed more than ok with this expla-nation and did little to comfort me or help me otherwise.

As I came up to Pentire Point, I took a moment to stop and gaze out over the sea. The lunar rays bounced off the still waters, making something so deadly look so so beautiful. Did I do everyone a favour and just end it all here? My life was nothing but a shitty mess of dot to dot being placed in one foster home to another. I was a drain on the system and beyond psychological help. Would it be easier to just not exist anymore? To find my mum in the afterlife and live my happily ever after there.

A single tear rolled down my cheek, surprising me. I'd not cried about my mum for years but being back in the position of fight or flight again, it was only natural her death would spring to mind.

I came home from school one day to find my mum and dad shouting at one another in the kitchen. The block of flats we lived in was small and dingy and I could hear their argument as soon as I opened the door to the building.

Dad didn't work, as such. His work involved finding men for Mum...to earn money with. At that age, I didn't understand it all. Mum had told me that her job involved making people happy and they paid her money for doing that. Of course, the stark reality of it only became clear as I got older. By the time I was twelve, I knew the full seedy ins and outs of prostitution and pimps and it only served to fill me with more hate and bitterness aimed towards my so-called dad.

Their argument that day escalated into physical violence. That was nothing new—he'd hit Mum before. I'd spent many nights helping her hold bags of frozen peas or sweetcorn to her face. But this was different. I heard the crack of her skull from inside my bedroom. I wanted to run out and see if she was ok, but I knew from experience to just stay hidden when they were arguing.

Mum hadn't made a sound. She normally kicked and screamed and yelled at him but this time there was nothing. I knew it was bad. I hid under my bed and waited for what felt like hours. Not a single noise could be heard except that of my own ragged breathing.

Convinced my dad had left, I dared to open my door just a little bit to see if I could help Mum tend to her injuries. When I saw her face down on the kitchen floor, a puddle of blood and little bits of something around her head, I cried and ran to her, yelling her name. I ran straight through the thick, sticky blood and shook her as hard as I could to wake her up, but it didn't work. I climbed up onto her side and pulled her hair back from her face to see a sight that still haunted me now.

One of her eyes dangled down her cheek like a bit of stringy cheese with a lump on the end. A massive indent caved in the side of her head, bits of broken skull, tissue, and what I now knew to be brain matter, all congealed into a disgusting mess.

I screamed, frightened by the sight and also realising that Mum was never coming back. I'd never see her Bambi eyes full of love and warmth and her smile would never take the ice out of my soul again.

"I wondered where you were, you little shit," Dad said, stumbling through from their bedroom with a bottle of whiskey in one hand and a bloodied bat in the other. "Come here."

I scrambled off Mum's body, falling backwards into her blood. "You killed Mummy!" I shouted at him, somehow getting to my feet. "You're a bad man."

He took a swig of his whiskey and glared at me with a malicious grin. "You have no idea, little doll. Now come here. I can make some use out of you."

I ran for the front door, which he'd stupidly left unlocked. I bolted down the corridor towards the stairs, screaming and crying for someone, anyone, to open their door and save me. When I heard his footsteps stumbling behind me, I panicked and rushed down the stairs, my legs not cooperating quick enough. I ended up falling down two flights of stairs and breaking my left leg.

Dad scooped me up, put a hand over my mouth, and said, "Shut your noise unless you want to end up like your pathetic mother."

On instinct, I bit him. I bit his fingers that hard his blood sprayed into my mouth and a chunk of his flesh fell onto my tongue. He hollered a string of profanities, but it worked—he let me go. By this point, the commotion had made some of the buildings occupants finally open their doors. Two men grabbed hold of Dad and wrestled him to the ground, cable tying his hands behind his back before calling the police and an ambulance.

A kind old lady brought me a blanket and a sugary drink and sat with me until the paramedics arrived. When I heard a blood curdling scream from above me, I knew someone had found Mum. I thought my nightmare was over. It had only just begun.

CHAPTER EIGHT

I pushed all of those thoughts to the back of my mind, wiped my tears, and carried on walking. Mum had been dealt a rough hand in life and she'd kept on going no matter what. I could at least honour her memory by staying alive and battling whatever came my way.

Just concentrating on putting one foot in front of the other, I surprised myself with how quickly I came across Port Isaac. As I thought about Tintagel and my plan to end up there in a few short hours, I realised I didn't want to be around people.

Throughout my life, people had done nothing but hurt me, lie to me, use me for their own gain, and broken me into pieces. Even my own father had wanted nothing to do with me until he thought

I could make him a few quid. Teachers had ignored my obvious state of neglect, police officers just wanted me off their shift and passed on to the relevant authorities, and the relevant authorities were just as corrupt and dark as the people they were supposed to save me from.

My foster families had been a slideshow of abuse and neglect, and the one friend I thought I'd made in this whole twisted world turned out to want nothing more than to laugh at me and enjoy my utter humiliation. I literally had no one to turn to. No one.

As it dawned on me that I'd been fighting a losing battle all along, desperately clinging onto any ray of hope of finding happiness, I let my tears free and changed direction. I didn't need to be running towards a different town full of yet more let downs and disappointments. I needed to be heading towards something positive and liberating, somewhere I could truly be happy.

The only person I could rely on was me and if my world didn't extend beyond me then so be it. At least I couldn't hurt myself or let myself down. There was only one place that would give me the solace I needed—Bodmin Moor. Pretty much in a straight line from Port Isaac, I turned my back on civilisation and marched towards my beautiful new future in the great outdoors.

I reached the edge of the moor just as the sun broke through on the horizon, signalling the start of another glorious summer day. My legs ached and my feet were sore. Walking across fields in the middle of the night wasn't my brightest idea. I'd stood in cow pat, tripped over molehills, and fallen over hidden holes in the ground, but I'd made it. I could rest at last.

A small copse of trees provided the perfect shelter for a few hours kip. I picked my way through to the densest part and cleared the ground of twigs. I could see no human rubbish which was excellent news—it meant no one came through here, at least not on a regular basis. The noise of a cockerel singing its early morning song sounded around the empty countryside, giving me an over-whelming sense of peace of and tranquillity. This out here, was soul food, the exact thing I needed to stitch myself back together.

I put my bag down on the ground and jiggled things around inside it so I could use it as a pillow. I settled down on my left side and closed my eyes, falling asleep almost instantly.

A soft tickling sensation across my face roused me from my sleep. I opened my eyes to see two huge green eyes staring at me and whiskers brushing against my cheek. A gorgeous black and white cat stood in front of me, purring, its tail up in the air like a flagpole.

"Hello," I said, reaching out and stroking its head. "And what are you doing?"

It touched my nose with its own and then turned around, showing me its ass and rattling the end of its tail. I giggled and stroked it. I'd never had so much as a goldfish, but I adored animals. They held such compassion and unconditional love, it baffled me. I wished I could view the world as simply as they did sometimes.

After a few minutes of me fussing it, the cat decided to lay down next to me, curling up next to my bag and against my chest. I didn't complain in the slightest. For the first time in a long time, I actually went to sleep with a smile on my face.

CHAPTER NINE

W hen I woke again, the cat was still there. It had obviously woken at some point because it was laying on its other side. That filled my heart with more love and joy than anything ever had. It didn't know me from Adam and yet it had chosen to stay with me. A whole world surrounded it, waiting for it to explore the beauty, and yet this kind little soul chose to keep me company as I slept.

The earth felt warm beneath me, heated by the June sun all day, but the slight chill in the air told me it would be setting soon, and another night would soon be upon me. Time to make some decisions. Did I stay here a little while longer or did I move deeper onto the moor? I glanced over at my feline friend and smiled. I didn't want to move and wake him or her. I would stay until the cat left me.

My throat felt as dry as the desert, but I knew if I reached for the water in my bag, the cat would wake and leave. As much as I knew that would happen eventually, I didn't want it to be because I'd forced it. I turned my thoughts to Marsha and Roger. Did they know I'd gone yet? Had anyone even missed me at school today? Having left my phone at Marsha's, I felt such a sense of relief and freedom from not having it on me I wondered why I'd ever wanted one in the first place.

Not being tied to an electronic device made way to enjoy the simple, beautiful things in life, such as the company of a strange cat. Or the sound of crickets chirping as the sun set. Things that were taken for granted and overlooked every single day in place of a virtual world that bred nothing but bullies and hate.

Some time after dark, the cat finally rose to its feet. It stretched out its legs, meowed at me, and trotted off into the night. It wasn't skinny by any means which meant it most likely had a home where someone loved it. I smiled to myself and finally sat up, quenching my need for water. I didn't feel hungry in the slightest, so I didn't bother to open any of my food. No point in eating it just for the sake of it.

I stood up, brushed myself down and guided by moonlight again, moved on. I emerged from the trees into the wide-open plains of the moor. I knew all the local legends about 'The Beast of Bodmin Moor' but I paid little attention to them. There were so many stories to prove its existence and just as many to disprove.

Personally, I felt it more than likely. I'd studied pictures, videos, and reports. Some of them were obviously domestic cats, but others were clearly something else. When the skull of a big cat was found on the edge of the moor a couple of years back, that kind of cemented the truth for me. Whether anything was still lurking around was another question.

Dartmoor Zoo claimed to have released puma's back in the eighties which would mean at least two generations of them had lived up to now. Whatever the case, if my end was to be a grisly, bloody death by a big cat, then so be it. It would just about be the perfect ending to my life. I smiled as I realised it really would be like mother like daughter if I died a gory death too.

I ambled across the uneven ground carefully.

Now away from civilisation, I had no need to keep up a hurried pace. The last thing I needed right now would be an injury. The silence out here on the moor was so profound, it bordered on eerie. Combined with the moonlight and how vulnerable I was being out in the open, I shuddered as I wondered if a pair of glowing green eyes were watching me from the long grass, waiting to pounce and end me at any given moment.

My destination for the evening's journey was a small area of woodland and trees east of King Arthur's Hall. Thanks to my keen interest in the supposed beast that lived out here, I knew where various landmarks were along the moor and would use them as my map. A small river ran just south of the woodland, it was remote, and provided perfect shelter.

I walked for what felt like hours, my feet and my legs soon complaining of the exercise once again. When I skirted the fence of King Arthur's Hall and saw my destination in the distance, I found my second wind. With no idea of what the time was, I felt nothing but free. That alone gave me so much happiness.

When I finally reached the trees, and saw how pitch black it was inside, I decided the clever thing to do would be to wait until daylight before venturing inside. I'd made it this far under moonlight and stars, the last thing I needed was to injure myself right as I reached the end. I could afford to sit on the treeline and wait for daylight. It's not like anyone would be walking by here anytime soon. My only company would be nocturnal insects and animals.

I sat down with my back against one of the trees and groaned in delight. My feet were throbbing and I was fairly certain I could feel a blister or two forming on my heels. My thighs ached like I'd done a hundred squats. I scolded myself for letting my fitness levels drop these past few months. I'd felt so comfortable and relaxed at Marsha's that I'd felt no need to continue with my daily jogs.

In the past, my sole intention of keeping fit had been for situations like this. Whenever social services shipped me somewhere new, I never went with the thought of 'this could be my forever home' but with the thought of 'I wonder how long I'll stay here' or 'I wonder where I'll be this time next month'. As a result, making sure I was in top shape, ready to flee at a moments notice, had been my highest priority.

When I was placed at Marsha's though, I knew

instantly things were different. This would be somewhere I could stay for more than a couple of months. Instead of my usual 'I wonder where I'll be this time next month' I thought 'I wonder how I'll mess this one up'. And here I was, messing it all up. I wasn't stupid enough to believe I wouldn't be found, it was only a matter of time, I knew that, but being out here gave me the perfect opportunity to make the most of the time I would have to myself.

Geraldine, my social worker, would be absolutely livid. Every time something went wrong it was always my fault. Even when I told her the truth about abusive foster parents, it was always somehow my fault. I'd even come to wonder if she cared more about her statistics and perfect KPI's than she did the kids she looked after.

But for now, I didn't need to worry about that. It would be weeks before they found me and that would give me more than enough time to clear my head, set myself straight, and be ready to jump back into the murky abyss of the foster system.

I leaned my head back against the tree and sighed. Thoughts of my father filtered in from somewhere and I couldn't help but wonder what had happened to him. Had he gone to prison? Had he been to rehab and turned his life around maybe?

Or was he still the same bitter, twisted person? Did he regret what he'd done? Was he dead?

As I pondered over the options, I realised that actually, him being dead was probably the best option. If by some miracle he'd managed to turn his life around and become a nice person, I still knew his capabilities, the darkness that lurked deep inside him. I'd never be able to forgive him for killing my mum, no matter his state of mind at the time.

There was a lot to be said for the whole nature versus nurture argument. I had every justification under the sun to be a copycat of my father, but I had no desire to be like that. It wasn't in my nature. Yet he was evil right down to the core. He was born a rotten apple and just soured more and more as life went on.

From what I did know of his upbringing, he'd been born to a wealthy family, had opportunities galore handed to him on a silver plate and yet he chose a life that was the exact opposite. His family disowned him and as a result, I had grandparents out there as well as two aunts and three uncles, that I had never met and likely never would meet. All because of his selfishness and the shadows he wanted to live in.

I hoped, if he was dead, that he could see all the suffering he'd caused and would be remorseful, maybe even help direct my life in a good way, to make up for the sins he'd committed and the nightmare I'd been forced to live as a result.

Out of the corner of my left eye, I caught movement along the empty moor. I turned my head and almost gasped in surprise. Limping along the vast landscape was nothing other than a lone horse.

CHAPTER TEN

The lunar light cast him in beautiful shadows, making his grey coat look almost pearlescent white. Even from this distance, I could easily tell he was a he. The crest in his neck, his body, the tell-tale sign underneath his stomach, he was every inch a stallion in his prime.

As he moved, his muscles rippled, making him look absolutely spectacular. This moorland wasn't horse territory though. What was he doing out here all alone in the middle of the night? And how badly was he injured?

Just like every other little girl, I'd dreamed of having my own pony when I was younger. I'd spent hours poring over horse books, learning about all the breeds and different disciplines. Many days had been taken up daydreaming about show jumping on a magnificent Thoroughbred or doing piaffes and effortless passage on stunning Andalusians.

This horse was clearly neither of those. Under the silvery light, he looked to be a chunky sort, possibly a native breed. The way he hobbled on one of his front legs though really concerned me. I carefully rose to my feet, intent on getting as close to him as I could to try and gauge his injury better.

I knew he couldn't be wild. There were no wild horse herds on Bodmin, and he was far too big to be a Dartmoor stallion. Plus, he looked far too well with his gleaming coat to be anything but an escaped domestic horse. That meant I should be able to get close enough to him to be able to potentially help him.

As carefully as I could, I tip toed along the tree-line, watching him for any signs of him having heard me moving. He'd come to a stop at the small river to the south of the trees and was taking a drink with his rear end facing me.

Stepping out of the shadows, I moved towards him. I managed to make around six feet before his head shot up, his ears twitching back and forth. I froze, my heart pounding. On his left shoulder, I could just make out a dark streak running down his leg. His knee looked to be pretty swollen too.

Now around thirty metres from him, I could tell he was a Connemara and an absolutely stunning example of the breed at that. Considering he was entire, and where his injuries were, I guessed he had escaped from his field. Someone would be missing him in a few short hours when they woke up to go and feed him.

"Hey, boy," I whispered, taking another step towards him.

He snorted and turned to face me. He pricked his ears so far forward they were almost touching at the tips.

"You look pretty beat up there," I said. "Looks like you need some help."

He stamped his good front foot on the ground and tossed his head up and down.

"Ok, ok," I said, holding my hands up and slowly sinking to the floor.

His entire body quivered and trembled—he was ready to flee at any second. I didn't want to cause him alarm nor give him reason to potentially hurt himself even more.

For several minutes I sat there, simply looking up at him, admiring his natural beauty. He didn't falter in his attention on me for a second. Just as I began to wonder how long we were going to be taking part in this stand-off, a rabbit popped up a few feet in front of him. By the time I'd realised what it was, he'd fled, his tail high up in the air and his hooves thundering across the ground.

By the time dawn broke on the horizon, I was more than ready for some sleep. My stomach grumbled at me finally and I gave in and ate a biscuit of my emergency rations. A biscuit didn't sound much but this stuff was awesome. It increased in volume when mixed with liquid which meant as soon as it hit my stomach, it swelled and filled me up nicely.

I finished the last of my water and wandered down to the river to refill my bottle. The water quality of the De Lank river was renowned for being exceptional. The source of it was right here on Bodmin which meant nothing flowed up, only down. I wasn't stupid enough to drink it neat though.

Filling the litre bottle, I carried it back to my bag and fished out my iodine drops. I read the instructions in the breaking dawn light. Five to ten drops per litre of water. Closer to ten if the water source was still or the water was cloudy. Closer to five if the water was flowing or clear. I decided to go for the middle ground and added seven drops.

I had to then wait five minutes, thread the bottle so the rim was free from bacteria and such as well, and then wait a further thirty minutes before the water was drinkable. I decided after threading the bottle, which simply meant turning the bottle upside down and unscrewing the lid until water leaked from all around the cap, then turning it back the right way, I would have a nap.

As I waited to thread the bottle, I scanned the horizon, looking for the Connemara stallion. I couldn't see him at all. I hoped wherever he'd gone, he'd find his way home and that his injuries weren't too bad.

Dawn fully broke out over the moor, giving me a glorious scenic view of orange rays spilling out over the plains, basking everything in a bright sunshine. The birds were in full song and the heat from the sun rise was already making the ground mist after a damp night.

I threaded my bottle, looked inside the trees, and decided it was time to rest. I could fully see inside now daylight had broken. After scouring the area carefully, I chose my spot at the north end of the trees. Any walkers or animals would stick to the river and the further away from people I was, the better.

The north end of the trees sat parallel to a derelict barn and dry stone corral. I would investigate them later on when I woke up. After all, a solid roof over my head would be better than trees but for now, the trees would do.

CHAPTER ELEVEN

I woke sometime in the afternoon. The sun had moved around but its heat was still borderline intolerable. I felt surprisingly fresh and well rested. Eyeing up my iodine cleansed water, I braced myself for the bitter taste. As the water flooded my mouth, I found myself pleasantly surprised. It had a bit of tang to it but was more than drinkable.

Carefully, I rose to my feet, listening out for voices, dogs barking, or any other indication of human life. Satisfied I had no immediate unwanted company, I grabbed my bag and slung it over my shoulder. I wanted to investigate the derelict barn. Perhaps a quarter of a mile to the west of the trees, it wasn't far at all from my current spot. It had its own barrier of trees around it which would provide me with even more cover.

I peeked out of the tree line, looking left and right to see if there were any little dots on the horizon indicating humans. It looked all clear so I stepped out, shoulders square and head held high, pretending I was just out for a regular stroll.

As I crossed the grass, I kept an eye out for the stallion, wondering where he could have gone to and hoping he wasn't further injured. I could see no hint of him whatsoever. Disappointment rose inside me and I couldn't help but feel a little bit sad. I'd not been near a horse in years and I did miss it, even if the memories of it were somewhat tarnished.

At the age of ten, I'd been placed in a foster family home down in Newquay. I was the sixth addition to their family and I'd had such a good feeling about them. I was the fourth girl to be added but not the youngest. One girl, Emily, was six. The other two girls were twelve and fourteen, Molly and Joanna.

The dad, David, had been every little girl's dream of a perfect father. He spent time with us watching girly movies, he helped us plait our hair, joined in with tea parties and dressing Barbie dolls, and he even baked cakes. Absolutely delicious, mouth watering cakes.

After I'd been there for a month, David said I could join the reward chart. I'd been so excited I nearly weed myself. Once a week on a Saturday, David took the girls horse riding but only if they'd been well behaved during the week.

The mum, Karen, was caring for twin boys, both still infants and feeding from the bottle, so she appreciated David keeping us older ones entertained. My memory of my first time sitting on a horse was something that would always stick with me. Not because it was so thrilling and enjoyable, but because it was my first inkling that something wasn't quite right.

David picked me up and put me on the saddle. I'd expected that as the pony was huge but apparently the best one for beginners to learn on.

As I sat in the saddle, David put one hand on my bum and the other between my legs. "You need to sit nice and deep," he said, pushing me into place.

His hands lingered for a little longer than necessary, but I ignored it. The other girls didn't seem phased by him at all, so I kept quiet. Maybe it was just how you had to be shown how to sit. Once

I'd learned how to sit, he wouldn't have to touch me like that again.

The next four weekends, I gritted my teeth through having David 'place' me in the saddle.

"Good," he said. "I think you've cracked the correct sitting position. Excellent, Blue. Really well done."

I'd beamed like anything, absolutely ecstatic that I'd been given some rare received praise and also wouldn't have to be positioned in the saddle by him anymore. The next week, however, was a little more interesting.

"You're going to learn to canter," David said. "And you need to learn to rock your hips in time with the horse's motion and rhythm." He stood at the side of the pony and placed his hands on my hips. "Just relax and let me show you." He then pushed my hips backwards and forwards, grinding me against the saddle. "That's what you need to do."

I completely freaked out, jumped off the pony on the other side to where he stood, and ran around the back of the stables, crying. All it did was bring back memories of the last home I'd been in where the man did nothing but try and touch the girls all the time.

Joanna came around after me and put her arms around me. "It's ok. It's not that bad."

I remember looking up into her green eyes and asking, "What's not that bad?"

"What he makes us do," she said, brushing some of my hair back from my face. "If we keep David happy then he keeps us happy."

"But...but he...he touched me...it's wrong."

She flashed me a sympathetic smile and hugged me. "It can feel good sometimes. The first few times are painful but he's really nice and gentle about it."

I frowned. "It didn't hurt."

"Of course this didn't hurt. I'm not talking about this part hurting."

I froze, my heart stopped dead. "What hurts?"

Her cheeks flushed pink and she started fiddling with her ponytail. "When you finally make love," she whispered.

My jaw dropped. I shook my head. "You're lying."

Her forehead creased into a frown. "I am not."

"You just fancy him, that's all."

She shrugged her shoulders. "Fine. Don't believe me then."

As Joanna returned to the stables to go and

ride, I thought about what she said. There was no way he would *do that* with her or anyone else but his wife. He seemed far too nice. My reaction had just been remembering things from my old home, nothing more.

I pushed it out of my mind and tried to carry on as normal. Two or three more weeks passed, David showing me how to rock my hips when cantering and me ignoring the raging memories trying to make me run.

However, the next night, after everyone had gone to bed, I woke up desperate for a drink. My glass was empty, so I crept out of my room and down the hallway to the kitchen. My room was the furthest away which meant carefully tip toeing past everyone else's.

As I passed Joanna's room, I heard whispers coming from inside. I couldn't help but stop and listen.

"Good girl, Joanna, yes, just like that. Pretend you're cantering across the field on Barney. Sit nice and deep in the saddle. Good. Yes."

I froze. My heart backflipped several times. I couldn't be hearing this right, surely? I reached out for the door handle and debated my options. The smart thing to do here would be to not open the door. Not Joanna's door at least.

Two doors down on the right, Karen was sleeping in the twin's room. Even my social worker didn't believe me about the last guy so why would this be any different? I quietly made my way to the twin's room and ever so carefully opened the door. To my surprise, Karen was awake and feeding one of them in the rocking chair.

"Hi," she whispered, smiling. "What are you doing up at this hour?"

I put my index fingers to my lips in a shush motion and beckoned for her to follow me. She glanced down at the baby, still sucking the bottle, and shook her head.

"Please, Karen," I whispered.

She pursed her lips and slowly rose from the chair, keeping the bottle in place and the baby happy. I grabbed her hand and tiptoed back to Joanna's room.

"Listen," I whispered, as quietly as I could whilst pointing at the door.

Karen stepped a little closer to the door. I heard David saying something about nice and deep again. Karen's face paled.

"Take the baby," she said, plonking him in my arms before I could protest.

She burst through the door like a stampede of wild horses. I'll never forget the look on her face. Joanna screamed and covered herself with the duvet whilst David scrambled for his dressing gown. Lots of yelling and throwing of things ensued before the police came to take David away. When the social workers turned up, Karen's hell became even deeper. David had been sexually active with all three girls, even six-year-old Emily.

Joanna, on the way back to her room to fetch her belongings, narrowed her eyes at me and said, "I told you I wasn't lying. Look what you've done, you've ruined everything. Karen hates us, especially you. It wasn't even your secret to tell."

From that day on, any secrets I found out, I kept to myself. If I told people, they didn't believe me, and if I let them find out for themselves, then I'd only be to blame and resented as a result. I literally couldn't do right for doing wrong. Story of my life.

CHAPTER TWELVE

The derelict barn was just that—an abandoned dry stone building. The roof was intact though and old straw lined the floor, some of it black and mouldy, other parts ok if a little dry and dusty. An old wooden ladder perched against the back wall, leading to an upper floor. I really wanted to see what was up there, but my gut told me to stay firmly planted on the ground. The last thing I needed right now was to fall through a rotten floor and break my leg.

Deciding this would be a better place to stay than the woods, I sorted through the straw, chucking the mouldy bits outside and piling the better parts up into the back corner as a sort of soft chair/sleeping area.

By the time I finished, my stomach had started grumbling at me again, so I indulged in another biscuit. I settled down for an afternoon nap, hoping that by the time I woke, the moor would be empty of walkers and explorers so I could do some exploring myself.

Twilight. A beautiful time of day. The mix of pastel colours glowing above the earth were extraordinary, every single day. Purples, blues, and yellows painted the evening sky and I could do little more than stand and stare at it. This was the exact medicine I needed to piece my soul back together.

From where I stood, at the side of the old oak tree outside the barn, I had a perfect view of the river to the south. Just as I wondered if I'd ever see the Connemara stallion again, he reappeared, peeking out from the left of the small woods I'd stayed in last night. He must have circled around and come back to the same spot. Had he been there all day?

I watched him, his ears moving back and forth

constantly, listening to the evening insects coming alive and looking for any danger that may be lurking. He limped over to the river and started drinking, his rear end facing me once more. I went back to my bag and dug out my tube of Savlon. It was the best antiseptic stuff ever and I swore by it. If I managed to get close enough to him, he definitely needed something to stop his wounds becoming infected. If I could even clean them.

Watching him carefully, I started making my way towards him. I kept myself in the open so he could see I posed no threat. Only predators would use the cover of trees to creep up on an animal. I was surprised his owner hadn't caught him and taken him back home but whatever the circumstances regarding his mysterious appearance up here, I wasn't going to complain.

He finished drinking before I had even gotten anywhere near him. Looking out over the horizon in front of him, he was either ignoring my presence or hadn't yet realised I was here. Considering horses have almost three hundred and sixty degrees of vision, I opted for the earlier option. Roughly sixty metres or so out, I decided to not startle him.

"Hey, boy," I said, calling out to him softly.

He turned his head, looking back at me, his ears pricked.

I took a couple of steps towards him which made him turn around, so he now faced me head on. His head up high and his whiskey brown eyes pinned on me, I knew whatever move I made had to be the right one. If he ran again, I'd likely never see him again.

A scene from The Horse Whisperer sprang to mind and I decided to try it. I had nothing but time out here. I sat down and watched him. My eyes never faltered from him once. After what felt like an age, he took a step towards me, bobbing his head up and down.

Resisting the urge to jump for joy, I bit my lip and waited him out some more. It took him twice as long to take a second step, but the second step became four steps, with him dropping his head to snatch at some grass.

I contained an excited squeal. He was curious. This was actually working. I thought about laying down but then realised that's what predators do—hide in the long grass, peering out over the top, so I stayed put.

Hours ticked by at a definitive stalemate. He stayed the same distance from me, slowly grazing his way back towards the trees, but always with an eye on me. His skin twitched around his wound, telling me that bugs were trying to get at it. It needed tending to asap.

With my legs going numb and my bum already having lost feeling, I knew I needed to move. I'd made such progress with him though I really didn't want to.

"Hey, boy," I said. "I'm just going to walk around a little bit. You're making me lose the feeling in my legs."

He snorted but carried on munching, still keeping a close eye on me.

As carefully and as slowly as I could, I rose to my feet, stretching out my muscles as I did. It felt so good, I couldn't help but groan with pleasure. The stallion though, he didn't move an inch. I breathed a sigh of relief.

I walked around in a big circle, flexing my legs and ankles and decided to be a little bit sneaky, just to satisfy my own curiosity about his curiosity. As much as I wanted to move towards him, I understood the moves needed to be his and on his terms. I knew from personal experience that the more someone tried to force themselves on you, the more you resisted, even if it was perfectly innocent and friendship based.

In light of that train of thought, I turned my back on him and walked back towards the barn. I wanted to look behind me so badly to see if he was following but I knew if I did, that would be it, ruined. He needed to want to follow me without realising it was exactly what I wanted him to do.

When I reached the oak tree, I took advantage of the shadows and finally turned around. I ran my finger up and down the tube of Savlon, hoping and praying he'd come close enough so I could treat him.

To my utter surprise, he had followed me, although he had allowed more distance to come between us. That didn't matter though, the main thing was he'd taken steps in my direction. That was huge and I really wanted to do some sort of celebratory dance or at least jump up and down to release some of the pent-up excitement inside me.

I sat down again, leaning back against the tree, and watched him. He snatched a mouthful of grass then ambled closer, stopping about fifty metres away. He carried on grazing, still careful to keep me in his line of sight.

Wondering if talking to him might help relax

him, I started rambling on about me and my life, airing out all my dirty laundry for all animals within earshot to hear. He didn't seem to mind in the slightest. I studied how he reacted to certain tones of voice. Whenever I spoke soft and quiet, he took a step closer. If I spoke normally, his ears twitched back and forth, and he stayed put. I didn't dare raise my voice to test his reaction to that.

"You like peace and quiet, hey, boy?" I said, borderline whispering. "Me, too. Not had much of it in my circus of a life. Kinda makes me appreciate moments like this."

I sighed and rubbed my eyes. Another cloudless night gave the moon full access to shine down on us, highlighting my way back to the barn for some sleep.

"You've worn me out for the night, boy," I said, as softly as I could. "I'm going to hit my straw bed for some sleep. I hope you don't stray too far."

I stood up, carefully, and headed back to the barn. My straw bed fell perfectly in a strip of moonlight, almost like it was being highlighted for me by the heavens above. If anyone was up there watching me, I hoped like anything that they'd give me a break and let me do some good, even if it was just tending to an injured horse.

I fell asleep, watching the stallion graze. He'd stayed put and not followed me further which disappointed me a little but he was still watching me. For the second time in three days, I fell asleep with a smile on my face.

CHAPTER THIRTEEN

I woke up to a snuffling noise. Blinking the sleep out of my eyes, I looked around, half dazed, to see the stallion stood under the trees outside the barn. Not the oak tree, the other trees closer to the barn, closer to me. He was sniffing the ground, blowing little clouds of dust up as he searched for food.

"Hey, boy. Good morning," I said. "Busy night eating your way up here, huh?"

He flicked an ear in my direction but that was all I got. I frowned. Did I dare move? When I saw him pick up a piece of mouldy straw, put it in his mouth, and then spit it back out, I realised he was hoovering up the flakes of straw from where I'd thrown all the bad stuff outside.

I grabbed a handful of straw and held it out to him. He snorted as if to say 'nice try'. Careful not to rustle my bed too much, I crawled towards him on my hands and knees, still with a handful of good, clean straw.

He allowed me to get within around twenty feet of him before he squealed and cantered off. I sighed and resisted the urge to face palm myself. Refusing to give up, I placed the straw where he'd been foraging and retreated back to my corner. I expected to wait hours for his return but to my sheer delight, and surprise, he wandered back over within a matter of minutes. I presumed the lure of the straw was what did it.

Whatever did it, the fact he was eating what I put out for him meant there was some basis of trust forming. He could have run off, disappearing completely, or he could have chosen the grass to eat, but he didn't. He chose to risk coming near me to eat the straw. If I could build on that then I'd be able to clean his wounds and hopefully make him better.

With his nearside facing me, and him only being metres away from me, I could see his injuries better, especially in the daylight. He had two cuts —one on his shoulder and one on his knee. The one on his shoulder looked pretty superficial, but it had bled a fair bit. The one on his knee however seemed particularly nasty given the swelling around it. Flies were already swarming around the congealed blood, making him flick his foot every so often to get rid of them.

I needed to tend to that knee first. Glancing at my water bottle, I had just over half a bottle left which would be more than enough to wash away the dirt and dried blood. But of course, I hadn't even managed to get within six feet of him yet.

"Was that good?" I asked him, as he ate the last piece of straw.

To my utter amazement, he took several steps towards the barn for a lone piece of straw on the ground near the entrance. Excitement buzzed all through my veins and my heart raced like a race-horse. Would I finally get to touch him today maybe? With no time restraints or commitment restrictions, I felt like the possibilities out here were endless. Just me and this gorgeous horse, all alone, trying to figure each other out.

I took another handful of straw and very slowly pushed it towards him across the floor. He flicked his ears forwards, eyed me up for a split second, and then to my absolute surprise, he pawed at the straw with his good leg, moving it back towards him so he didn't have to step inside.

"You clever devil," I said, grinning like anything. "That's sneaky."

He twitched his ears back and forth and the gleam in his eyes almost seemed to be as if he were laughing at me. I studied his colouring, totally in love with him already. He was a dappled grey, but the softest most gorgeous dusky colour of grey. With his dark mane and tail as well, he actually looked almost...

"Blue," I said, smiling. "I think you can share my name. I'll call you Blue."

He picked up a piece of straw and chewed on it, nodding his head slightly as he chewed on it. I knew the nodding was only something from eating but I could pretend he was nodding in response to my statement.

Feeling bolder, I dared to move a foot or so closer to him. He put his head down, ears pricked, and snorted, but most importantly, he didn't move. If he moved, it would be like taking two steps back. I restrained myself at this point. I'd made a move and he'd been ok with it. It was now his turn to make the next move and I would stay put until he did.

When he finished the straw at his feet, he looked inside the barn at the massive pile I'd made. He bobbed his head up and down and stomped his good foot on the ground.

"Oh no, Mr Blue," I said, smirking. "If you want some more, you can go get some more. I'm not your slave."

He pinned his ears back and stamped his feet again, pointing his nose at the straw.

I shook my head. "Nope. Your turn to move."

He snorted and shook his head, making his mane go all wild and fluffy. Then with a swish of his tail, he turned around and ambled back to the trees. *Damn it,* I thought to myself. I really thought the straw might have lured him in.

"Where are you off to?" I said, watching him walk away.

I hoped like anything he wasn't going to leave but if he did, who was I to stop him? Someone answered my hopes as he came to a stop under the shade of the closest tree, resting a hind leg and lazily swatting his tail at the flies pestering him without mercy.

The mid-morning sun had some serious heat to it. I dreaded to think how hot the day could possibly get if the temperature kept rising. With the sun being out and the moor such a beautiful place, I knew for a fact that people would be exploring the vast beauty out there, despite the sweltering heat.

Thankfully, the open side of the barn where I had made myself a home happened to be in the shade. Either pure luck or thoughtfulness from whoever built it. I definitely wouldn't be venturing outside until the sun had set, that was for sure. I eyed up the rickety old ladder and wondered again what could possibly be upstairs.

"No time like the present," I said, clambering to my feet.

Blue pricked his ears forwards but didn't move. I tested the bottom few rungs with my hands, making sure they weren't going to easily give way or about to collapse. Happy they were safe, I carefully eased my weight onto each one, testing the higher ones with my hands. I couldn't help but hold my breath each time I stepped up onto the next one.

By some miracle, I made it to the top without incident. I poked my head up and looked around. Bales of hay were up here, at least fifty, bottles of water, tarpaulins, old leather harnesses, buckets, and feed bags. I felt the board in front of me with my hands and hoisted myself up onto it, sitting on it and gazing around the space.

The hay bales had my first interest. If it hadn't gone mouldy, I could throw a bale down for Blue. And make myself a proper little bed. Fairly certain the floor must be good to be holding all this weight, I walked across to the hay, still a little tentative just in case I found a weak beam. Some strange white bags were hanging from the wooden roof beams. I squinted my eyes and managed to read 'Drypak Silica Gel' on one of them.

"That's so clever," I said, grinning like anything.

The hay would be as perfect as the day it was thrown up here. The silica gel would draw moisture out of the air and therefore stop the hay going mouldy. I took three bales and threw them over the edge of the floor. They landed with a thud at the bottom and I hoped and prayed I hadn't scared away Blue.

Upon investigating the water bottles, which were covered in about an inch of dust, they were huge five litre bottles of branded water. The expiration date had long passed but that meant nothing for water. I grabbed two of the dozen bottles and hauled them over to the ladder. I fished through the rest of the stuff and found nothing really much of interest. I nabbed a bucket, as that would come in handy for Blue to drink out of.

Then I thought about it and took a second bucket for washing his wounds. I put a bottle of water in each bucket and then made two trips up and down the ladder with each one. When I finally came back down, mightily pleased with myself with my haul of goodies, Blue was stood at the entrance to the barn, eyeing up the hay.

I carried a small flick knife with me wherever I went, for protection as well as other uses, so I dug it out of my bag and used it to cut the string on one of the hay bales. Super soft and meadow sweet, it fell apart into slices, just like it should.

Blue's brown eyes lit up and he started chewing even though he had nothing in his mouth. I pushed the hay a little towards him but not far enough that he could avoid stepping inside to eat it.

"Come on," I said. "You want it, you come get it. That's the deal."

I grabbed one of the buckets and keeping myself against the wall of the barn, edged my way outside. Blue stood and watched me every step, then as I emerged outside, looked at me and blinked, as if he were calling me stupid.

"What? I'm not the one who's skittish here."

I poured some of the water into the bucket and washed it with my hand, giving it a good rinse to get rid of the build up of dust and cobwebs. Satisfied that even I would drink out of it, I took it back inside the barn and placed it near the hay before filling it up. The instant I moved far enough away, Blue stepped forwards and drunk the entire bucket in about a minute.

"Someone thirsty, huh?" I asked.

He kicked the bucket over with his good leg and bobbed his head up and down at me.

"You want more?"

I slowly approached him, talking to him all the time. He didn't flinch once. I bent down and picked the bucket up and still, he didn't move. As I poured some more water in, I felt a soft muzzle sniffling through my hair. My heart skipped a beat and I grinned like a Cheshire cat. He'd touched me, of his own accord. He'd made contact with me because he wanted to. This was a fantastic day.

CHAPTER FOURTEEN

My biggest urge had been to reach up and try to stroke his face, but I refrained from doing so. I took his gentle snuffles as a thank you for the hay and water and retreated back to my corner. When he started eating the hay, he chose to move fully inside the barn, in the shade, and appeared nothing but chilled and relaxed.

I felt like I'd just discovered aliens, or a foreign language, and I wanted to run and tell everyone what had happened. Then it dawned on me that I had no one to run and tell anything to. In a matter of days, my world had changed from worrying about Archie and the tricks the little shit might try and play on me to worrying about making friends with a strange horse. It went without saying which world I preferred.

With my stomach grumbling yet again, I ate another biscuit and found myself needing a nap soon after. I cut open another hay bale and used it to fluff my bed of straw up. The instant I sank into it, I closed my eyes and fell asleep.

I woke up at some point during the late afternoon. The heat had started to fade and the sun hung low in the sky. Blue stood in front of the hay, his head dangling just above the floor with his bottom lip drooping, his eyes closed, and a back leg resting. If only I had a camera. Taking a picture of this right here would be a picture I'd want to treasure forever.

My time with him was limited, I knew that. It could come to an end at any given second and there would be nothing I could do about it. This strange little bubble we'd created between us though was something I didn't want to let go of. I'd become rather addicted and attached to the plucky little stallion. He'd given me a reason to live, a reason to want to do something, a reason to feel good and happy.

But ultimately, he belonged to someone else and would be found soon enough and taken back to his immaculate stable with his rich owners. Until then though, I could pretend this was our life and ignore the real world outside of our small, idealistic one.

"Hey, Blue," I whispered, stretching my legs out.

He flicked an ear forward and then back but otherwise didn't acknowledge my movement. I wondered if it would be too brave to try and address his injuries. Looking at the state of his knee, it couldn't really be left any longer. Not without going to get some help. I didn't want to do that as it would mean my inevitable trip back to social services but if I had to in order to help Blue, then I would.

I stood up and waited for him to react. Nothing. I smiled to myself as I wondered if he'd stuffed himself so full, he'd gone into some sort of food coma. I'd done similar myself over the years. Whenever I'd been on the run and picked up by the authorities, I'd cram every last little bit of food into me that I could, then fall asleep as my body struggled to cope with it all. One time I'd eaten so much I'd thrown most of it back up but after living out of rubbish bags for three weeks, everything tasted like heaven and I'd wanted it all there and then.

Making my way over to the other bucket with the second bottle of water inside, I picked it up, making the handle rattle. Blue opened his eyes briefly then closed them again. I washed the bucket out, tipped some water in and headed back to the sleeping beauty. I grabbed my Savlon and took off my socks. They needed washing anyway so would be more than ok for washing his wound. I turned them inside out and then sucked in a deep breath.

With the bucket and antiseptic cream in hand, I approached him. I sat down on the floor and dipped my sock in the water.

"Who's a good boy, Blue?" I said, reaching my hand up to touch his leg.

I held my breath and waited for the explosive reaction. As my fingertips met his silky soft coat, I almost shrieked in delight. He didn't move an inch. I'd done it. I had managed to calm a skittish horse. It was such an amazing feeling and my heart swelled with pride at the fact that this beautiful creature trusted me. Me, the messed up runaway kid who couldn't get anything right.

I spoke to him all the time, telling him what I was doing and why, made suggestions to him as to how he might have done this to himself, and tried to keep him calm and relaxed. It was only when I picked off a massive clot of congealed blood that he woke up. He lowered his head and sniffed my hands. My instincts told me to freeze, in case he bolted or bit me or something, but I fought against them and carried on cleaning his cut.

When I got rid of the clot, I could see the cut right across his knee bone. It was deep, but not bone deep. I cleaned it out as best as I could, even getting my little finger in there to get the little bits of dirt out. He didn't flinch once.

I opened my Savlon tube and spread a good amount onto my index finger. Still talking to him in a soothing voice, I dabbed it into his wound. After a couple of seconds, he bobbed his head up and down and lifted his leg in the air.

"I know it stings but that's a good thing, means it's working. It'll feel so much better, I promise."

I put my free hand on the front of his leg, and he placed his foot back on the floor. I cooed to him and told him what a brave boy he was. Amazingly, he let me finish applying the cream to the rest of his knee.

"We good to do your shoulder?" I asked him, putting my hand on his shoulder.

He moved away from me and snorted.

"Ok, ok. We'll do that one later or tomorrow then. We got the worse one."

He licked his lips and started chewing. Then he wandered over to his water for a drink and started munching hay again.

I felt like I'd climbed Everest and sailed back down the other side.

CHAPTER FIFTEEN

I sat up all night, telling Blue about what made me run out here in the first place. He listened, his ears moving back and forth at the sound of my voice. He nodded his head every now and again, even if it was to pull hay apart, which made me feel like he was listening.

"The moral of the story is don't trust people," I said, letting out a long sigh. "Which is kind of ironic considering I want you to trust me, but I'd never hurt you, Blue, you know that, right?"

He snorted and munched on the hay, his eyes half closed with peace and pleasure. I leaned back against the warm bricks and sighed. Where did I go from here? At the moment the one thing tying me to this exact place was Blue but once he'd gone, what was my move then?

I stripped off my clothes and unfolded my Scrubba bag. Luckily, thanks to the bottled water, I didn't have to sit by the river in my birthday suit and wash my clothes. I unwrapped my soap and cut a chunk off of it, letting it dissolve into the water before I added my dirty clothes. Once I put them in, it was a simple case of scrubbing the rough textured sides of the bag together which would act as an old-fashioned washboard. It was a marvellous invention and one I'd never be without.

The sun had set hours ago, leaving a crescent moon hanging in a clear night sky. The air was humid and sticky which meant my clothes would dry fairly quick. As I placed them outside on the grass to dry, an idea struck me.

I gathered up the string I'd cut from the hay bales and made myself a makeshift washing line, tying one end to the nearest tree and the other end to a rusty bolt that stuck out from the barn wall. I threw my clothes over it and decided to give myself a strip wash whilst my underwear dried.

Emptying the bucket I'd used to clean his wound, I refilled it with clean water and used it to wash my face and under my arms. Baby wipes would clean more intimate areas.

After I'd freshened myself up, I sat on the intact hay bale, on top of my bag, and tried to ignore the very uncomfortable feeling of being naked. This was the only part I really hated but carrying extra clothes just wasn't worth the hassle and space they took up.

I checked my underwear every few minutes, willing a blast of heat to come from somewhere and dry it in an instant. Of course, nothing like that happened and I just had to wait it out. Thankfully the cool night breeze was enough to make it wearable after an hour or so. Prancing around naked on a moor under moonlight made me feel like some kind of witch.

With my underwear back on and feeling a little more human, I sat back on the hay bale and chatted to Blue about Regan.

"He's absolutely gorgeous," I said, sighing. "No one could look at him and find him unattractive. But of course, he's nowhere near as gorgeous as you."

He blew some dust from his nose and carried on chewing, nudging bits of hay he didn't want out of his way.

"He didn't seem to care about my past either and that's rare. Then again, I thought that of Izzy too. People are fickle, Blue. All nice to your face and then stab you in the back the instant you turn around."

He turned his head to look at me, his brown eyes relaxed and gleaming as he carried on eating the hay. To my sheer surprise, he walked over to me and stood in front of me, his head drooped so his ears were level with my face.

"Hey, boy," I whispered. I lifted my hand slowly and rubbed the centre of his head. He stood there for a couple of seconds then bobbed his head up and down. "What are you trying to tell me?"

When he moved his head, I hadn't moved my hand and after a few seconds I understood what he was doing and what he wanted.

"You're a clever little minx, aren't you?" I said, giggling.

He stopped moving his head and left me to scratch up and down his face. After just a few scratches, my fingers were covered in dirt and my nails a murky brown colour.

"Someone needs a bath," I said. "Or are you just trying to make me need another wash?"

He sighed and continued standing there after

he'd finished his mouthful of hay. I continued scratching his face, gradually moving my hand from the centre of his head up to his ears and down his cheeks, curious if he preferred any other areas being itched.

I even tickled under his chin which he seemed to like. He half closed his eyes and sighed as I tickled him like a cat. After I'd scratched literally all of his head, I moved my hand to his neck, attempting to scratch the crest of his neck.

At that point, he woke up, nudged my arm away, and ambled back to his hay.

"That's ok," I said, more than happy with what contact he'd allowed. "One scratch at a time, hey boy?"

I sat there watching him, as he shifted his weight onto one back leg and rested the other, eating his giant pile of hay. He had just come to me for attention, for fuss, that was a huge step. Grinning like an idiot, I fetched my nearly dry clothes in, got dressed, and went to sleep for another night with a massive grin on my face.

CHAPTER SIXTEEN

I woke to bright sunshine outside, another cloudless day from what I could see of my limited view. Even though my stomach hadn't grumbled as of yet, I decided to indulge in another biscuit. I wasn't oblivious to the fact that my energy levels were depleting, and I was sleeping more as a result.

As had become the norm over the past few days, I looked towards the barn entrance for Blue. My heart jumped. He wasn't there. I scanned the area outside that I could see from where I was but I couldn't see him. My stomach lurched and upset filled me. Had he really gone?

I turned to my left to reach for my bag for my biscuit and startled with shock. Blue was laying down behind me. I'd woken up all but cuddling the wall and couldn't see behind me. Of course, I hadn't expected in a million years to find him so close to me in such a vulnerable position.

He'd nestled himself against the back wall and seemingly created himself a hole in the straw so when he laid down it rose up around him. His nose was only about a foot away from me, his neck and head stretched out towards me.

Oh my God I thought to myself. This was absolutely amazing. I wanted to reach out and touch him, but I knew if I did it would wake him up and the magical moment would be over. Not wanting to disturb him at all, I put the idea of my biscuit on hold. As quietly as I could, I laid down on my left-hand side so I was facing him and just stared at him.

He looked so peaceful, calm, and relaxed. What had happened to him in his life to make him as nervous and mistrusting of people as I had become? He didn't look old. He was well muscled, his coat shiny, every inch the epitome of peak physical health. I had no idea of how to tell a horse's age by their teeth and the likelihood of me getting anywhere near his mouth was slim to none anyway, but I was fairly certain he couldn't be in double digits.

As I laid watching him, I couldn't help but smile. His legs started twitching and his ears flicked back and forth. A minute or so later he grunted. Was he dreaming? I'd seen cats and dogs moving and making noises in their sleep. Was it possible for horses too?

With his soft muzzle only inches from me, I had to resist a lot of temptation to reach out and touch him. I knew the velvety softness of a horse's nose and I missed the feel of it more than I realised. Still, I'd figured by now that patience was key here and when he wanted me to touch him, he would let me know, like last night.

It wasn't long before I felt my eyelids drooping and the heavy pull of sleep luring me back into peaceful dreams. With Blue enjoying his own peaceful rest next to me, I happily gave in.

I woke again sometime later. It took a few seconds for me to remember Blue had been laid down next to me and I immediately looked for him. He wasn't there but the indentation he'd left on the straw was. I grinned. At least I knew I hadn't dreamed it.

Lifting my head, I looked down to the entrance to see him stood with his pile of rapidly diminishing hay.

"Hey, boy," I said. "Did you have a good sleep?"

He moved an ear towards me and swished his tail. I stood up and stretched my arms and legs. Blue pricked his ears in interest but kept eating. Feeling bold, I moved towards him, telling him I wanted to look at his knee. He kept on chewing and didn't bother at all.

Refilling the wash bucket, I cleaned his wound again and reapplied some more Savlon. He didn't bother at all. I touched his shoulder and watched him for a reaction. Nothing. I dipped my fingers in the water and rubbed at his shoulder wound. Still nothing.

I kept on chatting to him as I cleaned his shoulder and dabbed some antiseptic cream onto it. "There we go," I said, grinning. "You're all fixed up."

He turned his head towards me, and half closed his eyes, as if he were smiling. That was all I needed.

CHAPTER SEVENTEEN

I decided later that day to take a wander around the other side of the barn, just for a change of scenery. As I wandered around the drystone wall corral, I heard a noise behind me. I turned around, half expecting to see a person, but found myself staring at Blue.

"Hey, you," I said, smiling at him. "What are you doing?"

He stood there, looking at me all innocent.

"I just came for a look about," I said, starting to walk around. "You want to see?"

He cocked an ear in my direction and followed me.

"You know I don't have any treats, right? You're doing this all because you want to."

He swished his tail from side to side and ambled around next to me. I stopped. He stopped. I started walking. He started walking.

"This could be fun," I said.

I stopped again, and so did he. I approached him from his nearside and put my hands on his neck. His eyes filled with worry for a moment but after a couple of seconds, he dropped his head and started licking and chewing.

"Who's a good boy?" I said, running my hands up and down his neck. I didn't want to push my luck too far and risk freaking him out. "How about a scratch?"

I ran my fingertips over him, scratching him in various places to see if he had any favourite spots. Watching his reaction absolutely filled me with joy. I could literally see in his face he was thinking how strange it was but how nice it was too. When I started scratching around the centre of his chest, he cocked his head to one side and started twitching his top lip.

"Is that nice?" I said, laughing. "What about double trouble?"

I put one hand on his withers and the other on the centre of his chest, scratching both spots at the same time. He stretched his neck out and lifted his head high in the air, twisting his top lip up. I couldn't help but laugh. I kept scratching him until my fingers ached.

"I'm sorry, boy," I said. "My fingers are hurting."

He sighed and turned around, then to my amazement, started nuzzling my shoulder. Was this his way of giving me something back?

"You are such a sweetie," I said to him, rubbing the centre of his head.

I wandered back to the barn, with Blue in tow, and wondered where to go from here. He was clearly enjoying interacting with me and I wanted to build on that. There was something unique forming between us and I wanted to embrace it as fully as possible.

Our routine over the next few days was the same. I'd wash his wounds and reapply some antiseptic. Then we'd wander around the back of the barn and have some fun in the corral. Whenever he did something I wanted him to, he'd get a scratch in his favourite place.

It was either my imagination or the actual

truth, but he seemed to do what I wanted him to do before I'd even asked him. I'd literally just have to think it and he was already acting on it.

As we spent more time together, I soon had him trotting and cantering on command, backing up, and doing various patterns, all from me just using my voice and thinking what I wanted of him. Every time I said 'good boy', he'd come to me for a scratch, then wander back out and carry on with what he was doing previously. He seemed to live for love and praise.

The real turning point for us came one night when a storm hit. It had been humid and muggy all day and when I saw the grey clouds hanging low at sunset, I knew we'd be at least getting some rain. I went up into the loft and threw down several more hay bales, intending to build a wall out of them so part of the open front was partially blocked off and would give some shelter.

Blue paid little attention to me as he munched on his pile of hay. Literally within five minutes of me finishing the 'wall' of hay, the heavens opened, and typically the rain came into the barn. I grabbed my bag and with a shriek as the rain turned into hail, I ran behind the hay wall for shelter.

I stared at Blue with raised eyebrows,

wondering what the hell he thought he was doing braving the hail with his bum turned to it.

"You can eat your hay from in here," I said, pointing to the space next to me. "Hardly like you're going to starve, is it?"

He snorted and then moved to exactly where I'd pointed. The storm blew on for hours, never relenting once. When the thunder and lightning came, I realised we were in for a sleepless night. I cuddled up next to the hay wall, but I couldn't get comfortable. I'd gotten used to my little 'nest' over in the opposite corner.

As I battled to find a comfortable position to sleep, Blue gave up eating, finally, and with a grunt, laid down on the straw. I laughed at him wondering if he'd eaten himself into a food coma again. I fidgeted something chronic, unable to get comfortable. After a few minutes, Blue propped himself up on his shoulder and looked at me.

"What?" I said. "I can't get comfortable."

He gave me a blank stare and then laid back down.

We repeated this process another three or four times—me fidgeting, him sitting up and staring at me, then laying back down. The next time he sat up, he touched his chest with his nose, and then laid back down.

"Are you saying what I think you're saying?" I asked him.

He sighed and closed his eyes.

My entire body filled with nervous excitement, I crawled over to him and gently laid my head on his neck. When he didn't move or react in any way whatsoever, I fell asleep comfortably, smiling yet again.

CHAPTER EIGHTEEN

Blue was nothing short of amazing. In just a few short days, his shoulder wound had all but healed up and his knee was doing really well. Washing it twice a day and applying Savlon after each time seemed to be working a treat.

Wherever I wandered to, he followed me like a dog. I wasn't convinced how good of a guard dog he'd be but I appreciated his company nonetheless. I didn't stray far from the barn and only ever at night to avoid spying eyes. I hadn't quite worked out if Blue was rideable or not and without any tack or a riding helmet, I wasn't sure I wanted to experiment.

We took a wander to King Arthur's Hall one night. The moon was nothing but a sliver in the sky and masked by heavy rain clouds. It was almost pitch black on the moor but for some reason I decided it would be a clever idea to go for a walk.

I could see the fence in the distance and kept my eyes peeled on it, intent on making it there without fault. Instead of following me like a puppy, Blue kept at my side, his shoulder level with me. His big swinging stride made it difficult for me to walk and not run but we managed to stay in time with each other.

Feeling brave, I put my arm on his withers and grabbed a handful of his mane, allowing him to guide me over the uneven ground. He stepped around big rocks and waterlogged areas like he knew the place inside out.

When we reached the hall, I climbed onto the stile, ready to go exploring within the boundary. Blue stomped his foot and shook his head.

"I just want to see it all in darkness, boy," I said. "Imagine what it would have been like all those years ago."

He pinned his ears back and pulled a face at me, swishing his tail in annoyance.

"Ok, ok, I get the picture," I said, sighing in defeat. As I started to climb back over the stile, he sidled up to it, blocking my exit. "How am I supposed to get back over there when you're in the way, doofus?"

He bobbed his head up and down, snorted, and stamped a foot, almost as if he was telling me I was being stupid. I stood up on the stile, ready to push him away so I could get down, and then realised what he was doing.

"Oh my god," I said. "You can't be serious."

He stood there patiently, looking all pretty as he gazed out over the dark landscape.

"You better look after me, Blue, because if I fall off and hit my head and die, I'm coming back to haunt you."

He snorted and pawed the ground.

Biting my lip, I held my breath as I grabbed onto his withers and slid my right leg over his broad back. Tingling excitement rushed through me like a shot of adrenaline and my heart pounded like crazy against my ribs. This couldn't be happening, could it?

I plunged my fingers into his thick mane and held on for dear life. He walked forwards and I couldn't help but let out a little shriek. Of all the things I had ever done in my life, this had to be both the most incredible and the stupidest. I'd never really learned to ride a horse and hadn't ever been back on one after David.

Somehow though, this felt like the most natural thing in the world. I relaxed and just let my legs dangle down either side of him. Whilst I was clinging onto his mane for dear life, I did my best to sit up straight and keep my chin up.

"If you look at the floor that's where you'll end up," is what David used to say.

Blue ambled around the perimeter fence of the hall at a steady pace. Seeing it from horseback, in the middle of the night, sent my imagination into overdrive. I wondered if Guinevere had really existed and what it would have been like to ride this land centuries ago. What would have actually been stood here?

I chatted away to Blue, telling him my wonderings out loud about women in beautiful dresses and knights in shining armour on galloping steeds. When we'd walked around the entire fence, he came to a stop back in front of the stile.

"What's up?" I said, frowning.

He put his head down and sighed.

"You're going to make me walk all the way back?" I said, giggling to myself. "You're mean."

I reached out for the stile with my left leg and

grabbed onto the fence post to pull myself off him very ungracefully. After I'd dismounted, he turned around and looked in the direction of the barn.

Giving him a good scratch in his favourite spot, I laughed at him. "You are so mean."

He nuzzled my shoulder and then nudged me which I took as a sign to get a move on.

As we walked back to the barn, I began to understand why he didn't want me on his back. The zig zag patterns he made, and the occasional sudden dodge of a hole or rock would have made it difficult for me to stay on.

I couldn't help but marvel at how intelligent and amazing this horse was. The longer I spent with him, the more I wanted nothing more than for it to be just me and him forever. We'd come together in the strangest of circumstances but had developed an intense bond and uncanny way of communicating. We seemed to be connected on a deeper level, almost spiritual. He knew my thoughts, without a doubt. Was this kind of connection even possible?

CHAPTER NINETEEN

I woke the next morning to find Blue laid flat
out on his side, no less than a foot away from
me, snoring. He was actually snoring. I giggled and
mentally cursed myself for not having my phone to
record this. Still, it would be a memory I would
hold forever, that I knew for sure.

My stomach growled alerting me to the need
for food. I only had one biscuit left which meant I'd
spent nine days out here so far. Nine fun filled,
soul fixing, heart warming days with this incredible
horse.

No food meant I'd have to go on the hunt for
some and that would be difficult to do with a giant
dog in tow. Even if I did it legitimately and bought
food from a shop, he'd still be hanging around

outside which was kind of noticeable, even to country folk.

I ate my biscuit and pondered my options. How could I make him understand he needed to hide whilst I sourced myself some food?

All of a sudden, Blue woke up, propping himself up on his shoulder. His ears were like radar antenna, twitching in all directions. Then with a huge grunt, he pushed himself to his feet and pulled a face at me with his ears back.

"What? Did you have a bad dream or something?"

He nipped at the air beside me, his teeth scraping together as he did. I stood up, shocked. I knew he meant business. My heart began to race and adrenaline poured through my veins. What was going on? What had he heard or sensed?

Walking out of the barn, he stood with his head up high, listening. I followed him out and waited next to him. I strained my ears but couldn't hear anything except early morning birds. He took a couple more steps and turned to the left, his attention focused on something behind the barn.

I still couldn't hear anything. His entire body started quivering and he lifted his tail. He was getting ready to run but from what? Not particularly wanting to be flattened by him when he decided to bolt, I moved out of his way and stood next to the hay bale mounting block.

Just as I opened my mouth to speak to him, I heard a shout from behind me. I peered around the side of the barn to see a quad bike flying this way, a couple of dogs running in front of it. A fair way out still, I could barely make out the person on it, but they were definitely heading this way. I ran into the barn and grabbed my bag, throwing it over my shoulder.

Blue spun around and trotted over to the hay bale, pawing at the ground. I didn't even think about it—I hugged my bag to my stomach, jumped on the hay bale and then onto his back. I threw my arms around his neck, leaning down over his withers, and closed my eyes.

My hands had barely clasped together before Blue took off with a spurt of energy that literally sucked the air from my body. I could hear nothing but the wind whistling in my ears and the thunder of Blue's hooves.

I clung onto him as he flew over the moor, zig zagging from side to side with the agility of a rabbit. If I hadn't been hugging his neck so tight, I'd have fallen off already. I didn't dare open my eyes. I trusted Blue and that was all I needed.

At various points when he changed direction, I heard the roar of engines, shouts, and barking dogs. Whatever Blue was doing wasn't working. We weren't going to escape. He couldn't outrun vehicles, not even a racehorse could do that.

We kept on going for what felt like ages. He was getting tired, I could feel it in him. His breathing was heavy and laboured and his pace had begun slowing with every stride. Beneath my hands, his chest was slick wet with sweat.

"Blue, easy boy. You're going to kill yourself," I said, scratching his chest as best I could through the damp hair.

He eased down to a trot, his sides heaving like bellows. I sat up and looked around to find three Land Rovers and two quad bikes coming at us from all sides. Four dogs were careering towards us, barking and snarling.

I stayed put on Blue's back, figuring it the safest place to be. Before I could even think, a gunshot echoed through the air. I screamed, "No!" and flung my arms around Blue's neck, desperate to keep him alive in any way I could.

Seconds later, a dart appeared in Blue's shoulder, little pink feathers sticking out the end of it. I plucked it straight out but as Blue stumbled beneath me, I realised it had already gotten to him. I tried to sit up but instead found myself sliding off him towards the floor, a streak of blood following me as a crunch sucked me into darkness.

CHAPTER TWENTY

W hen I woke, my head was pounding like hell. I went to move my left arm to put my hand to my head, but something stopped it from moving. Blinking the grogginess away, I focused my eyes to find myself in a room, strapped down to a table. My wrists and ankles were bound tight.

Panic surged through me. Where the hell was I and why was I tied up? I lifted my head to get a better view of the room but found myself crippled by a blinding pain in my left shoulder. I glanced over to see thick bandages covering it up.

Then I remembered the gunshot right before I fell off Blue. Had I been shot? Judging by the small red mark leaking through the bandages, I guessed so. Whoever would shoot a teenage girl and dart a horse? No one good, that was for sure.

I decided to study my surroundings as best as I could. I would find a way out of here even if it damn near killed me. The ceiling above me was wooden. Damp filled the air, invading my nose and making me feel ill. I laid my head down and tilted it back, trying to gauge the size of where I was.

When I saw a wooden wall staring back at me, inches from my head, I started to really worry. I bit my tongue through the pain of lifting my head and looked down towards my feet. A wooden door, just big enough for one person as an entrance and an exit. My stomach churned with dread. I was in a garden shed.

I heard a horse neigh from close by. Instinct told me it was Blue. I'd never heard him neigh but something in my gut told me it was him calling out. A desperate need to get to him filled me. His call was high pitched, frightened, shouting for help.

Biting the inside of my lip, I attempted to move my left arm, just to see how much use of it I would have. The instant I tried lifting it, hot searing agony hit me like a bulldozer. I clenched my fists and let tears leak from my eyes. The answer to that was no

movement. Strapped down to a table in a garden
shed with a bullet wound, this was a predicament
only I could find myself in.

"Think, Blue, think," I said.

Then it struck me. I'd watched a fair few documentaries about people being kidnapped and
murdered. The one thing everyone did that ended
up getting them killed quicker was scream and
create a fuss. All that did was annoy the perpe-
trator even more and make them see their victim as
nothing but something that needed to be taken
care of.

I needed them to see me as a fellow human
being, not an annoying fly to swat and kill. As I laid
there, I recalled what I remembered from when
they circled me and Blue. Five vehicles. That
meant at least five people. Four dogs. Two were
collies. I think one had been a Rottweiler but the
other I couldn't remember for the life of me. Quad
bikes and collies. Usually something found on a
farm. Collies were the A class dog for herding. But
Blue wasn't a sheep.

Taking into account the five vehicles, which
each needed a driver, and the fact Blue and I were
both shot, that meant at least six people. Unless
they were gangsters used to drive by shootings,

they couldn't shoot a gun and drive. I knew for a fact the quad bikes only had one person each. The Land Rovers could have easily contained at least four people each but if this was the criminal enterprise I now suspected, numbers would be kept to a minimum.

Six people and four dogs. That was my challenge. I had no idea where the hell I even was let alone how to raise the alarm for help. I smiled at the irony. This would be a new one—me actually going to the authorities willingly. With my past history of being a runaway though, would they even believe me?

I pushed the negative thoughts to the back of my mind. I couldn't allow myself to be defeated before I'd even gotten out of here. Voices sounded from outside and I could hear footsteps coming towards the shed.

A bolt slid across the door, the screech of the metal piercing right through my skull and making my headache ten times worse. As the door opened, daylight flooded the dingy shed, blinding me momentarily as my eyes adjusted.

"Well, well, well," said a male voice. "She's awake."

"Hello, poppet," said a female voice. "How are you feeling?"

I blinked furiously until my vision returned. A big burly man stood to my right. Dressed in a blue boiler suit covered in mud, a flat cap, and streaks of grease all over his weathered face, he really did look like a farmer. His hazel eyes were hard and emotionless and the flat stare he gave me actually gave me the chills. Suddenly my past foster homes didn't seem so bad.

To my left, a petite old lady with a slight hunch back started undressing my bandages. A pair of glasses perched on the end of her nose like a librarian and the woollen cardigan she wore over her flowery dress made me think of a grandma. Not that I had one of those.

"Thirsty," I replied. "Can I have a drink please?"

The man snorted. "No."

The woman looked at him over the top of her glasses and narrowed her eyes at him. "Fetch her some water."

"Water means she'll need the toilet which means more chance of escape," he said, his gravelly voice sending a shiver down my spine.

The woman rolled her eyes. "For goodness

sake, Colin. Just do as your damn well told before I tell Barry."

Colin muttered something under his breath and stomped back outside. Through my limited view of the open door, I could see a farmyard. Churned up mud, gravel, an open sided barn with an old tractor and straw bales, and some sort of evergreen hedge.

"I'm Edith," the lady said. "I do apologise for this little situation we have here."

"It's ok," I said, smiling at her. "Exactly the kind of thing I'd get myself into."

She chuckled as she removed the last of my bandages. "Healing nicely from the looks of it. I'm going to clean it so this may sting a bit."

I watched as she used a pair of forceps to pick up a gauze pad, dip it in water, and then scrub my shoulder with it. If I thought trying to move it had been painful. I was sorely mistaken. The pain from her touching the open wound had me seeing stars. Nausea swelled in my stomach. A deep ache accompanied the firing heat blazing through my muscles.

"Nearly done," she said. "You're doing spectacularly well. This antiseptic is a bitch but it's good stuff."

Even though that explained some of the pain, it didn't make me feel any better at all. Still, at least she was using antiseptic. I smiled as I thought about Blue. Had this been how he'd felt when I'd put my Savlon on his knee wound? No wonder he wouldn't let me touch his shoulder afterwards.

"Where's my horse?" I asked, trying to distract myself from the stinging in my shoulder.

"We both know he's not your horse, poppet," she said, putting a clean pad on my bullet wound. "But he is safe and unharmed. He's a tricky one, that one. Not the first time we've had to dart him."

"Can I see him?"

She laughed. "You're ballsy, missy, I'll give you that."

I grinned. "If you don't ask, you don't get."

"That is very true," she replied, applying a fresh bandage. "My dad used to say the same thing."

"I'm hardly going anywhere, am I?" I said, looking down at my shoulder. "I don't have anywhere to go to anyway."

"I must admit, I have been wondering what on earth a pretty little thing like you would be doing riding a wild stallion in the middle of the moor."

"Wild? He's not wild."

She tweaked her thin pink lips up into a smile.
"He may as well be. None of us can do anything
with him. Just before he escaped, he nearly killed
Colin." Her smile turned into a grin and she whispered, "Between you and me that wouldn't have
been a bad thing."

I giggled. "Not very friendly, is he?"

"He's a typical local I'm afraid. Doesn't like
outsiders or anything he's not familiar with. He
won't even eat his dinner without gravy because
that's all he knows."

I laughed. "Each to their own."

Colin returned then with my glass of water. I
smiled at him and said thank you but didn't even
get eye contact from him. He really didn't want me
to have this water.

"Untie her please, Colin," Edith said, undoing
my left wrist.

"Are you crazy?" he said, his voice rising by ten
decibels. "She's going to run."

Edith tutted at him. "Where is she going to run
to exactly?"

"Home. The police."

"You should pay more attention to the local
news. She's the runaway everyone has been looking
for. She's going nowhere."

Colin pressed his lips together so tight, his moustache nearly met his goatee. Without a further word, he yanked at the wrist restraint and let me free. As they undid my ankle ties, I thought to myself that was rather easy. The question still remained—now what?

CHAPTER TWENTY-ONE

A farmyard was the right guess. A big old farmhouse sat not a hundred yards away from the shed where I'd been kept, smoke pouring out of the chimney, chickens pecking their way through the muddy grass out the front, and two Jack Russell terriers laying around outside the door.

Six dogs. Not four, six. And ankle biters were the worst. I smiled to myself as I recalled a saying my mum had about my dad.

"He's like a terrier on a trouser leg, Blue. He just doesn't give up."

I'd never understood it until I'd met one of the little critters. Horrid things. It was thanks to one of them that my first attempt at running away had been thwarted and I'd been subjected to a further month of sitting in soiled clothes and living off bread and butter. I learned for the second try and crushed some of my foster mum's sleeping tablets into his food.

"I'm guessing you'd rather like a nice long soak in a hot bath?" Edith asked, gesturing for me to enter the house first.

I began to wonder if these people were cannibals or something. Were they wanting me bathed and fed before they killed me and ate me? This certainly was the most peculiar kidnapping I'd come across. Not that I'd experienced any previously but from what I'd seen on TV shows.

"That would be rather nice," I said, walking into a porch littered with muddy boots and shoes.

One of the terriers growled at me. I glared at it and stuck my tongue out. It jumped to its feet and started barking at me.

"Merry, shush," Edith said, silencing the wretched thing instantly.

I smirked at it and walked past. *One-Nil you little shit, one-nil.* I started to take my shoes off at which point Edith told me not to bother.

"I give up trying to keep this place clean," she said. "Take a left into the kitchen, dearie."

The porch opened up into a beautiful flag stone floored open plan room. The kitchen sat to the left, an old Aga in the centre and solid oak cupboards surrounding it. To the right a large red corner sofa curved around a giant TV. The delicious aroma of freshly baked bread hit me and in that instant I missed Marsha's house. I wanted to be back in my bedroom being teased relentlessly by the spawn of the devil. Was that being homesick?

But then again, if I was still at Marsha's, where would Blue be right now? I'd have never met him and that is something I definitely didn't want to even think about. In less than ten days I'd connected with another soul, but not a human, a horse. The bond we shared was so intense and profound, I couldn't imagine having something so special with another human.

We shared a mistrust of the same species and our friendship had been born from that. I felt honoured and extremely proud that despite his obvious abuse and lack of love, he'd found it within him to let his guard down and trust me. Did that mean there might be hope for me after all?

"Would you like some homemade lemonade?" Edith asked, gesturing for me to take a seat.

I nodded. "Yes, please."

The dining table was made from solid oak and clearly been here many years judging from the marks criss-crossing its aged surface. Edith went to the fridge in the corner and pulled out a big jug full of ice and slices of lemon. She poured me a glass and set it down in front of me.

"Thank you," I said.

"You're welcome. If you're fair with us, we're fair with you."

I don't get that impression from Colin, I thought to myself. "Can I see Blue please?"

She frowned and sat down opposite me with her own glass of lemonade. "Blue?"

My cheeks flared. "Sorry. It's what I called him. Felt wrong not giving him a name."

"It suits him actually. I like it." She narrowed her eyes at me and smiled. "Your name is Blue, isn't it? From what I remember hearing on the news?"

I nodded. "How long have you had him? He's in fantastic condition."

She cleared her throat and took a sip of her drink. "Not long. I think he's still pining for his last home. He managed to jump out of his field a few days ago. That's how you happened upon him. He won't be doing that again, that is for sure."

I smiled. "Made the fence taller?"

She snorted. "No. He's staying firmly put in his stable."

My heart skipped a beat. No. He would go spare. He loved the open space and freedom to roam around. All horses did. It was against their very nature to keep them locked away in a small wooden box. An overwhelming urge to find him and set him free almost made me act without thinking. However, I couldn't afford to put one foot out of place until I'd figured this situation out.

"Are you hungry?" Edith asked. "You look like you need a good meal."

"I could eat a horse," I said, laughing.

She winked. "That could be arranged."

A shiver went down my spine. Something in the way she said that made me think they probably had eaten a horse. "How many horses have you got here?"

"A few. We tend to...wheel and deal."

I nodded. "You're dealers?"

"So to speak, yes. I handle all the finances and the boys do all the graft round the farm and with the horses."

"Are they your sons?"

She nodded. "All five of them. Was interesting bringing them up on my own, I'll tell you."

Six people. I was right. "I bet it was."

"They're good boys though. Will do anything for their ol' mum."

"That's the way it should be," I said, smiling at her.

She cocked her head to one side and smiled back at me; a proper genuine smile that shone from her eyes as well as her mouth. "You seem like a good kid. What are you doing running away from home?"

I thought about lying for a split second and then realised I had no reason to lie. Edith didn't know me and after I'd figured a way out for me and Blue, I'd likely never see her again. Talking to strangers about my life seemed a whole different ball game than talking to someone I knew. There was a level of disassociation that came with talking to someone new that provided a level of comfort to a degree.

"I've not had a home in nearly ten years," I said, taking a sip of my lemonade. The bitter sweetness flooded my tongue and I found myself actually quite liking it.

"Orphan?"

"Kind of. Dad killed Mum when I was six. Nothing has gone right since then. In and out of foster homes, children's homes, emergency accommodation. Never stayed anywhere more than a few months."

"How come?"

I shrugged my shoulders. "Nothing worth hanging around for."

As I said that, the penny dropped. I had a reason to wait around now—Blue. My life had been completely upended in the last few days and I now couldn't see life without him. We depended on each other, we were each other's lifelines, and right now, I needed to be that lifeline for him and get us both the hell out of here.

"That's a real shame. Young girl like you should have a stable home and things to look forward to, not be wondering where her next meal is coming from and what disaster she needs to avoid next."

"I just carry on and deal with whatever is thrown my way. Not a lot else I can do."

She flashed me a sympathetic smile and then said, "How do you fancy a nice hot soak in a big bubble bath?"

I grinned. "I fancy the sound of that, that's for sure."

"Follow me," she said, rising from her chair and heading towards the stairs.

I followed her up the wooden stairs, noticing the shiny varnished finish to each step and wondering how slippery they might be. I'd have to be careful coming back down. I couldn't afford any injuries, not with Blue relying on me.

At the top of the stairs, the landing split left and right, four doors down each side. Straight in front of me was a white door that Edith opened to reveal a monstrous sized bathroom. When I saw the freestanding bathtub complete with gold feet in the middle of the room, I nearly squealed in delight.

"You have no idea how much I've wanted to always sit in one of those," I said, not even attempting to hide my Cheshire cat grin.

"You enjoy yourself, dearie. You've had a long, tough few days." She pointed out the towels and all the bubble bath and shampoo. "Can I wash your clothes for you whilst you have your bath? I can leave them outside the door once they're clean and dry."

I hesitated for a moment. With Edith being so welcoming, it really didn't feel quite real that I had been kidnapped. "Sure, if that's ok?"

"Of course. It's the least I can do. And I must apologise for the scene in the shed. I wanted to bring you in the house from the beginning but sometimes it's best to appease Colin than to fight him."

"I understand. Thank you."

Edith made her way out and closed the door behind her. As I stripped off and threw my clothes outside for her to wash, I couldn't help but understand how some people built relationships with their kidnappers. Edith was a very friendly, likeable lady and to think of her being anything but helpful and kind seemed peculiar.

I ran myself a wonderfully hot bubble bath and slipped beneath the bubbles, trying to formulate a plan of escape.

CHAPTER TWENTY-TWO

By the time I'd had a long soak in the bath, being mindful not to get my shoulder wet, Edith had washed and dried my clothes and laid them outside the bathroom for me. I surprised myself with how grateful I felt and wondered if this was the beginning of Stockholm Syndrome.

As I put my clean clothes on, the waft of freshly laundered clothes hit me and I found myself thinking of Marsha yet again. I'd never run away from anywhere and found myself thinking back to the family I'd left behind. Had I made a grave error in judgement this time? Potentially messed up the one chance I might have had at being happy?

I pushed the thoughts away. I didn't have time

to think about that now. My priority was figuring out this situation and how to get me and Blue the hell out of here. I headed back downstairs to find Edith in the kitchen preparing a joint of beef.

"Do you eat meat?" she asked.

I nodded.

"Roast beef for tea," she said. "My boys favourite."

"Do you need any help?" I asked, remembering that I still needed to come across as a human, not a possession.

"That's sweet of you but I'm alright, thank you. You should rest with that shoulder of yours." She nodded towards the sofa and the TV. "Go and help yourself. Put your feet up."

I faked a smile and did as she suggested, my mind whirring away with options and plans. I needed to get a good look around the place, see where Blue was, see where the possible exits were, and formulate from there. This had to be done logically.

Flicking the TV into life, I was surprised to see Sky TV at my fingertips. I automatically headed for the documentaries and put on a program about sharks. I had no interest in it really, but it was mindless, easy watching, and gave me the opportunity to occupy my mind with other ideas whilst seeming to look interested in patterns of hunting in various species of sharks.

A yellow teleporter rumbled past the window, flecks of rust speckled all over it. The front bucket was piled high with clean straw and I wondered if it was going anywhere near Blue. I watched it from the corner of my eye disappear around the side of the house. I didn't dare turn my head to follow where it went in case Edith was watching me.

I heard a horse neigh, but it wasn't Blue. Becoming more and more worried about him by the second, I chewed on my nails in a fruitless effort to calm my rising anxiety. I couldn't settle my mind from just wanting to find Blue and run.

My bet though was that every possible exit had been gated and padlocked shut. When I'd tended to Blue's injuries, I'd taken a guess that he'd jumped over something and hit himself on the way over. If I could figure out where he might have escaped from, it might be a way out second time around for him.

"I tend to eat after the boys," Edith said, clattering around in the kitchen. "I let them have their fill and then help myself to whatever is left. You can eat with me and afterwards I'll take you to see that horse."

My stomach jumped with excitement. "That's fine, thank you."

After she said that, I couldn't concentrate on anything, not even how to get out of here. All I wanted to do was see Blue and let him know everything would be ok. I would find us a way out of here if it damn near killed me.

None of the men spoke to me when they came in for tea. Edith told me to just ignore them so that's what I did. I carried on watching TV, forgetting about shark shows and indulging in The Big Bang Theory instead. Humour was definitely something I needed whilst I tried to calm the mix of adrenaline and anxiety churning away inside me.

Around six-thirty, the men headed back outside, chatting amongst themselves, and Edith called me to the table. I expected a slice of beef and maybe a handful of veg. When I saw how much food they'd left, I dreaded to think how much had been served in the first place. There was enough leftover to have meals from for the next three days.

"Help yourself, dearie. You need some meat on your bones."

I didn't hold back. Seeing this amount of food, let alone how good it all looked and smelled, after ten days of surviving on rations was like heaven. I was as happy as a duck in a puddle. Piling on mashed potato, peas, carrots, parsnips, roast potatoes, and finally three slices of beef, I knew I wouldn't be running anywhere tonight.

"I hope your belly is bigger than your eyes," Edith said, smiling at me. "We have a clean plate policy in this house."

I grinned at her and all but inhaled the entire plate. In less than ten minutes I'd eaten the lot. My stomach actually ached from being so full. I'd definitely be in a food coma soon, that was for sure.

"Shall we go and see that horse?" Edith said, rising from the table. "The sun is setting and dark falls quickly around here."

"Sure," I said, trying to sound as casual as I could.

"Follow me then," she said, toddling towards the front door.

The terriers didn't even bother with me this time, thankfully. Edith led me around the side of the house. A huge evergreen hedge, easily six foot tall, lined the edge of what I presumed was a paddock. A metal five bar gate with razor wire on top of it provided the only access in and out. As soon as I saw it, I knew that's what Blue had jumped over. I swear I saw spots of blood on a couple of the razor tips.

Edith opened the gate and ushered me through into a large field. It wasn't quite what I'd been expecting. I'd envisioned a field with some stables or maybe a field shelter. Instead, I saw a carefully constructed, well thought out set-up. A row of six stables lined the back edge of the field, each one with its own fenced area that reached over halfway across the field. Part of the fenced area was concrete, the rest grass. The same set up, with another six stables, sat on the right-hand side of the field, leaving a huge perfect square near the gate.

"Wow," I said, rather taken aback. "I've never seen anything like this."

"We deal with high end horses," Edith said, leading me across the field. "We can't afford to have them turned out together and possibly injuring each other in play. This way they're still in company and can reach over the fences for scratches and such but kicking and play fighting is out of the question."

"What if they eat all the grass in their bit?" I said, trying to guess the size of each one.

"They have nearly two acres each. If you look square on at one, you'll notice the fence fans out from the line of the stable wall. We give them hay all year round as well to help save the grass as much as possible."

As much as I hated to admit it, it was a very clever set-up and it looked professional and well cared for. I spotted a stable on the right-hand side of the field, at the very end, that had both the bottom and top door of the stable shut.

"Is that where Blue is?" I asked, pointing at it.

She nodded. "We have to close the top door, or he'll jump out. Little sod has tried it twice since he's been back."

I bit my lip to stem the flow of emotions rising inside me. He would be going stir crazy locked away in the dark, nothing to see and no way of seeing other horses. What the hell were they playing at?

As we approached the edge of his 'field', a loud crash sounded from inside his stable and the entire thing visibly shook. He neighed, but it wasn't a friendly nicker, it was a shrill scream for help. My blood ran cold, and my heart pounded against my ribs. A sheer desperation to calm him overwhelmed me and I couldn't help myself.

"You have to let him see," I said, ducking through the post and rail fence and running to him. "He's going insane."

"That's just his sedative wearing off," Edith said, following me. "Barry will be back shortly with his next dose."

I slid the bolt back on the top door and swung it open. When I saw Blue I gasped, my hands flying to my mouth. Tears instantly glazed over my vision. Drenched in sweat, he was almost black in colour, save for the white foam covering parts of his coat. His brown eyes, days ago so soft and peaceful, were wild and hardened over. He was shaking from head to toe.

Blood had smeared down his face and he also had red stains on one of his back legs. Parts of the stable wall had holes inside, chunks of the wood laid on his dirty bed. The smell of ammonia lingered in the back of my throat, almost choking me.

"Blue," I cried, my voice shaking. "Hey, boy."

His ears twitched and he turned to face me, his eyes softening just a fraction. Edith came to stand next to me and in that instant, the slight softness in his eyes vanished and he lunged at her, his ears pinned back, teeth bared, and a guttural grunt that made him sound like a wild animal.

"Whoa," she said, ducking down out of the way. "And that is why we keep this closed." She swung the top door shut again and slid the bolt across. "Not quite the horse you were riding two days ago, eh?"

"You have to let him out. You're sending him crazy."

"Sweetheart, that horse is crazy. There isn't nothing we're doing to make him crazy, trust me."

"Will you let me be alone with him?"

Uncertainty flashed through her eyes. "I don't know about that."

"You can stand at the gate and watch me. I'm not going to do anything but try and calm him down. Please?"

Edith sighed and pressed her lips together. "Ok. But any signs of funny business and you'll be spending the night in the shed."

I smiled at her. "Deal."

She pottered away, negotiating her way through the fence before ambling over to the gate. She leaned against it and watched me like a hawk. Eager to gain her trust, I lifted my hand and waved, giving her a smile too. She nodded her head in return.

I turned back to the stable and started talking to Blue. Carefully sliding the bolt back and reopening the top door, I kept in the back of my mind that he may well ignore me and revert to his basic animal instincts which he'd just shown Edith

"Hey, boy," I said, leaning over the door. "How are you doing?"

His sides were heaving and his head hanging low. I guessed the attack he'd just launched on Edith had left him with little energy. I checked the corners of the stable for food and water. Nothing. No wonder he was lifeless.

I looked at the pen next to me and spotted a chestnut right down the far end, grazing. I jumped the fence and pinched its water bucket and hay net, sliding them under the fence. Back on Blue's side, I dared unbolt his main door, talking to him about the amazing bath I'd had in the Victorian era replica bathtub.

The second I placed the water bucket down in his stable, he came over and drank from it, slurping as he struggled to take enough in at once. When he finally lifted his head, after draining the entire bucket, I showed him the hay net.

I expected him to snatch at it greedily, but he didn't. He stuck his head forwards and touched my face with his nose, his warm breath blowing through his velvety soft nostrils.

"Hey, boy," I whispered, raising my hand to tickle his chin. "I'm gonna get you out of here, I promise."

He nuzzled my hair, his top lip ruffling through it as if he were searching for food. I closed my eyes and giggled. The rush of happiness and peace had tears spilling down my cheeks and I knew without a doubt that I couldn't turn my back on this horse. We were soul bound.

I opened the stable door a little further so I could get inside and hang his hay net up. As I did, Blue pushed past me at full speed, knocking me to the floor. His hooves clattered against the concrete then thundered onto the grass. He let out an ear-piercing scream right as I heard the shot of a gun.

CHAPTER TWENTY-THREE

"Blue!" I yelled, scrabbling to my feet. I'd fallen onto my left shoulder and it throbbed with pain, but I ignored it. "Blue!"

I ran out of the stable to see one of Edith's sons coming towards the pen, a rifle slung over his forearm. Blue had come to a stop and was teetering on his feet. Then I saw the pink feathered end of a dart sticking out of his neck.

At least it wasn't a real bullet. He was alive. Dazed, but alive. I needed to get us out of here ASAP. The trauma he would be suffering because of this would be unreal. He couldn't take much more before there would be no way back for him. I couldn't, wouldn't, let that happen.

I thought Colin had been a big burly brute. He

had nothing on this guy. He was like a walking giant. Striding across the field in a dark green boiler suit with muddy green wellies on and a weathered face set like thunder, I wanted to run and hide.

"Get the fuck away from my 'orse," he said, pointing a finger at me.

I ignored him and ran to Blue, pulling the dart from his neck. "You can't keep him like this. It's cruel."

He bent over and came underneath the fence. When he straightened up, he narrowed his dark eyes at me. "My 'orse is my problem. You go back to my mam and do as you're damn well told."

I stood my ground. I'd met men like him time and again. "He won't be your horse if you don't feed and water him because he'll be dead." Blue tried to turn around, almost falling over in the process. "Look what you've done to him!"

"'E'll learn 'ventually that actin' up don't get 'im nothing but pain. If 'e be'aves, e'll get food 'n water."

Pick your battles wisely, Blue. Know when to fight and when to back away and strategise. One of my mum's sayings. She'd suffered a particularly nasty beating from my dad one night and I'd asked her why she didn't fight back or do something. That had been her reply.

Realising that this moment was not one to pick a fight, I backed down. My heart and soul shattered into a million pieces as I watched him use his gun to poke and prod Blue back into the dark, disgusting stable. When he bolted both doors shut, after taking the hay net out, I wanted to collapse into a heap of tears.

However, what made me want to collapse into a heap of tears also drove me on in my pursuit to get out of here by whatever means possible. I knew for a fact now that I was not leaving this place without Blue. Not even to fetch help. We'd either both leave together, or both suffer here together.

Edith didn't say a word when I reached her. She simply gave me a sympathetic smile and led me back inside the house. I offered to help her clean away after tea, but she declined.

"That shoulder of yours took a fair old knock. You need to rest it."

I sat back down in front of the TV and flicked on a Marvel movie. As I settled down, a mobile phone rang, the loud ring tone drowning out Thor's beautiful voice.

"Bloody man," Edith said.

I turned around to see her answering a black mobile.

"Hi, Mick...Yes, he's left his phone laying around again...Ok, no problem, I'll tell him. Bye."

That was like music to my ears. Someone made a habit of leaving their phone behind. That was exactly what I needed.

I heard Edith put it down on the table. As the night wore on and Edith's sons made their way indoors, Edith showed me to the guest room.

"They like a beer and to have a poker game or two before bed," she said. "Best if we stay out of their way. Especially after that little incident with Barry earlier."

I smiled and nodded.

The guest room was homely and pleasant. Pale blue walls, old white furniture, and a huge King size bed, it provided all the necessities I hadn't had over the past two weeks—a solid roof and a comfortable place to sleep.

I slipped beneath the duvet with my clothes on. I hoped and prayed that the phone downstairs remained there. Once everyone had gone to bed, I would grab it and call for help. With my head on soft pillows, a full stomach, and nice and warm, it didn't take long at all before I fell into a deep sleep.

When I woke, I panicked, but seeing it was still dark outside, I calmed my racing heart and gave myself a few minutes to clear the sleep fog from my mind. Very quietly, I tip toed over to the door and opened it, inch by inch, waiting for any squeaks or creaks. Thankfully, none came.

A clock on the opposite wall told me it was 2 a.m. Plenty of time to do what I needed to do. In my utmost stealth mode, I crept across the red carpet towards the top of the stairs. My heart pounded so hard against my ribs I was certain the noise of it would wake one of them.

Step by step I navigated the stairs, none of them making a noise. About halfway down, I bent down to see into the kitchen and spotted the phone still on the table. I bit my lip to contain the 'Yes!' that wanted to escape me.

I descended the stairs as quickly as I dared. Once at the bottom, I raced across the flagstone floor, holding my breath at the cold beneath my feet. Tapping the screen, I saw a request for a pin code come up.

Goddammit!

But then I remembered that didn't matter, I could still call the police. Urgency building inside me like a tidal wave, I dialled 999.

"Emergency; Which service do you require? Police, fire brigade, or ambulance?"

"Police," I whispered.

"Just a moment."

I turned around to face the stairs so I could see if anyone was coming down.

"Police, what's your emergency?" said a friendly female voice.

"I've been kidnapped."

"You've been kidnapped?"

"Yes. But I don't know where I am."

"What's your name?"

"Blue. I ran away from my foster home two weeks ago. I've been kidnapped and me and my horse need help."

"Your horse?"

"Yes. Please, just come."

"Can you remember any defining features about where you are?"

I sighed, impatience getting the better of me. "I'm on a farm somewhere. There's horses here. And six people. And six dogs. Please. You need to come now!"

"I have tracked your call and dispatched units to your approximate location but I need some help to pinpoint where you are exactly."

"I don't know!" I said, trying to keep my voice low. "All I know is there's a mum and five sons. Edith, Colin, and Barry are the only names I know. And that's all I know."

"Are you near any windows? Can you see outside for any landmarks or anything?"

I looked out of the kitchen window for a few seconds, squinting my eyes through the darkness. "It's too dark. All I can see is a hedge. The stables are behind it."

I checked over my shoulder to make sure no one had come down the stairs yet. The relief I felt when I saw an empty stairwell almost sent me dizzy.

"Please stay calm, Blue. I need you to stay with me on the phone. Do you understand?"

"They could come downstairs at any minute. I need to go. I need to go back to my room."

"Blue, listen to me. I need you to stay on the line with me, ok? My name is Kimberley. Tell me what you see in front of you."

My heart raced so fast the beats were almost one continuous rhythm. My throat had run so dry I could barely swallow. I'd broken out into a cold sweat and I couldn't think straight, let alone form a coherent sentence. I closed my eyes and tried to calm myself down.

"Blue, are you there?"

"Yeah," I croaked.

"Good. Tell me what you see in front of you."

I opened my eyes and instantly froze. "Oh shit."

CHAPTER TWENTY-FOUR

My little friend, Merry, stood in front of me, tail stuck straight up in the air, eyes pinned on me, and teeth bared.

"Blue," Kimberley said. "Talk to me."

"I gotta go," I said, putting the phone down on the worktop behind me. I made sure not to hang up, just in case she could pinpoint my exact location.

"Shhhh," I said, holding my hands out to Merry. "There's a good girl." Merry growled. "Boy. Good boy." Merry growled again. "Whatever the hell you are. Good...thing. Shush now."

I made a move to my left which the wretched thing followed, lunging forwards at me and snapping its teeth. "Ok, ok. We can be friends, right?"

I bent down, thinking if we were on the same level, it might calm her or him down. However, the instant I started moving, it growled louder.

"So what you gonna do, huh? Just keep me pinned here all damn night?"

It wagged its tail from side to side and came towards me again, still growling. I loved animals but right now I wanted nothing more than to kick this thing out of my way and get out. Apparently though, Merry had other ideas.

The longer I stared at the dog, the louder it growled. I figured if I broke eye contact, it might think it had won and leave me alone. So I broke eye contact.

Merry barked. Continuously. A proper terrier bark—high pitched and as irritating as a nettle rash. In less than thirty seconds, all six of them were up, moving around, and heading down the stairs. Edith came down first, rubbing the sleep out of her eyes.

"Blue, what are you doing?" she asked, padding over to me in her flowery dressing gown.

"Just getting a drink," I said.

"But you're dressed."

"I fell asleep in my clothes."

Her eyes fell on the worktop behind me, spotting the phone. When she looked back at me, a hardened glare fell over her face like an iron curtain. "Barry!" she yelled. "It's time."

Panic swarmed me. Time? Time for what? Edith grabbed the phone and hung up on the operator. Then she grabbed my wrist and marched me outside. Merry escorted her, snapping at my ankles. With nothing to lose anymore, I took great pleasure in taking a swing or two at the damn creature. I missed, unfortunately, but it made me feel better for a split second.

Edith marched me back over to the shed I'd initially woken up. She unbolted the door and shoved me inside. "You ungrateful girl," she said. "We'd have accepted you into our family."

Barry appeared in the doorway, his bulging frame struggling to fit through the door. Carrying a roll of silver duct tape, he bound my ankles and wrists and then sealed my mouth shut too. He handed Edith the tape and reached behind his back.

My fear notched up a hundred levels. When he pulled a handgun out of the back of his trousers, I fell over and scrambled across the floor to the corner of the shed. A sinister smile spread over his lips. He raised his arm, gun in hand. Seconds later, everything went black.

A screaming horse woke me up. I opened my eyes, my head absolutely on fire and throbbing like anything. I lifted my hand to the source of the pain only to find I couldn't move my hand at all. I was back on the table, strapped down, duct tape over my mouth.

Every time I blinked, searing agony shot through my temple like an electrical bolt of molten lava. My shoulder ached and out of the corner of my eye, I could see red smears on the bandages.

Footsteps sounded around outside, more than one pair.

"Steady, easy!" shouted a man. "They're traumatised. Don't rush them."

I heard hooves clambering up something. A ramp, maybe? Had the police come at last? I lifted my head, ignoring the cries from my shoulder, and looked at what I thought was the door. Except it wasn't. It was a wall. A corrugated sheet of metal.

What? I thought I'd been put back in the shed? I glanced around at my new surroundings to see I'd been stuffed in what appeared to be a wall cavity. Daylight shone through the underneath of the curved sheeting, allowing me to make out what appeared to be boxes, cardboard boxes. Where the hell was I?

I tried rocking the table from side to side but it was heavy and stuck fast. I made as much muffled noise as I could until my throat felt raw.

"We've looked everywhere," a male voice said. "No sign of her. Maybe she managed to escape."

"No," replied a female. "She's here somewhere. Keep looking."

I made as much noise as my throat and duct tape would allow but it appeared to not work as the footsteps faded away.

Time ticked by. I didn't know if it was minutes or hours but however long it was felt like an eternity. I heard another ear-piercing scream, and I knew it was Blue. Various shouts sounded through the air along with the scuffle of boots and hooves.

"Watch out!" someone yelled, before a thud hit the ground.

Hooves clattered along the gravel, a persistent neigh accompanying them.

"Get him back!" someone else shouted.

"I need my gun!" someone else yelled.

I started to really panic then. Gun, what sort of gun? They couldn't shoot Blue, they just couldn't. If he died, a part of me would die with him.

The hooves came closer, getting louder. Then they stopped. I heard heavy breathing and snorting coming from my left-hand side. Then hooves pacing up and down. Was that Blue? Did he know where I was? I made as much noise as I could, in case he was on the other side of the wall by some sheer miracle.

"Easy now," said a male voice, soft and gentle. "No need to be scared. We just want to help you."

Blue snorted and I heard him stamp the ground with his hoof.

"Don't corner him," said someone. "If you corner him, he'll fight back."

I started crying then in my frustration to just be heard. Blue stomped the ground again with his hoof.

"Wait!" someone cried. "He's trying to tell us something."

Come on, for goodness sake.

"Look," said a woman. "There's straw piled up against the inside of the barn, but do you see any straw poking out from the outside wall? Is this hollow?" she said, smacking her hand against the metal wall. "That'll be a yes then."

I heard hands running across the sheeting and people calling my name. A couple of minutes passed by before someone shouted out, "I've got a door!"

Daylight poured in as the makeshift door was wrenched open. Within seconds, the entire area filled with people, people who just wanted to help me and get me to safety. I realised then that actually, my species did have redeeming qualities. I'd shown Blue that people could be trusted and in some bizarre return of the favour, he'd allowed me to see the exact same thing.

CHAPTER TWENTY-FIVE

Everything that followed was just a blur. I was carted off in an ambulance thanks to my bullet wound and my head injury. I had asked everyone to let me see Blue, but they ignored me, more concerned with getting me to hospital. I hoped and prayed they didn't hurt him any more than he already had been.

Apparently, Edith had done a good job of patching me up. I had a concussion and a nasty cut from Barry's pistol whip, but other than that, I was ok. I had to stay in overnight for observation and they put me on a drip of antibiotics because of my shoulder, just in case.

Marsha came running into my room the instant

they said I could have visitors. "Oh, you, silly, silly girl! I've been worried sick about you!"

"I'm sorry," I said, bursting into tears. "I'm so sorry. Please don't hate me."

"I could never hate you," she said, squeezing my hand. "I'm just glad you're ok."

We sat and talked. I told her everything I'd been thinking and feeling. She listened intently and I knew I'd made a grave error in judgement. But that had led me to Blue, so had it really been an error in judgement or a blessing in disguise?

A knock sounded on the door and a middle-aged brunette woman in a beige trouser suit opened it. "Hi," she said, flashing an ID card. "I'm DCI Baker. Can I come in?"

I nodded. I figured this might come at some point.

"I appreciate you've had a tough time of it, Blue, but I really need to ask you some questions. Is that ok?"

"Of course."

I wanted to do anything I could to help with the investigation. I didn't know anything about what had gone on as of yet, but I guessed it wasn't just a case of them kidnapping me.

"I can't share details with you, but I need you to tell me as much as you can remember about what happened from the minute you first saw them."

I took a deep breath and recalled everything I could remember, right down to the stupid little dog that sold me out.

"Speaking of being sold out," Marsha said. "I think you have some people wanting to come and see you."

My happiness fell like a stone through water. "I'm not interested."

"They just want to say sorry, Blue."

I shook my head. "If you smash a plate and say sorry, does it put itself back together?"

Marsha shared a look with DCI Baker. "Well, no."

"There's no going back for me. That's a part of my past, including the people in it. I don't want to look back, I want to look forwards."

Marsha cleared her throat. "What shall I tell them? They're waiting downstairs."

I shrugged my shoulders. "Tell them I'll write them a letter."

Marsha grinned. "Touché."

DCI Baker laughed. "I'll leave you be now,

Blue. But don't worry about a thing. I have a feeling everything will work out just fine."

She winked at me and left the room, leaving me wondering what exactly she meant.

The doctors kept me in for two days, much to my annoyance. I was only allowed home on strict instructions for bed rest and Marsha did her utmost to ensure I stayed put. I didn't dare disobey her after the hell I'd put her through. When a knock sounded on the front door, I somehow managed to restrain myself from running down the stairs when I heard the friendly voice of DCI Baker.

A few seconds later, a knock sounded on my bedroom door.

"Come in," I said, hoping to God that I'd be given some good news.

The door opened and her familiar smile greeted me. "Hi, Blue. How are you feeling?"

"Like my shoulder has been ripped out and put back in the wrong place."

She laughed and sat down on the edge of my bed. "I have some news for you regarding Blue."

My heart lurched and my mouth ran dry. "Oh?"

"We found his original owners. He was stolen around six weeks ago from an Irish stud down in Truro. This particular gang have made quite a habit and a fair amount of cash from stealing high end stud horses and holding their owners to ransom. Blue would have been their biggest payday yet. Until you came along."

I smiled but couldn't hide the rising disappointment that I'd be losing him forever. Truro was only an hour away, but I knew how things like this went. Contact slowly faded into nothing once daily life settled back to normal and in a years' time I'd be all but a memory from another lifetime.

"When is he going home?"

"He went home when you were found," she said, patting my hand.

I bit back tears, blinking the water away from my eyes furiously. I didn't even get a chance to say goodbye. Goodbyes had never been my thing but there was something unfinished, unresolved almost, between me and Blue and I felt I needed closure on the time we'd spent together and the connection we'd shared.

"It's a good home, isn't it?" I asked, my voice trembling.

DCI Baker nodded. "The best. He has everything any horse could ever desire. A huge stable full of soft straw and meadow fresh hay, acres of lush green grass to run around in, and mares in the next field."

I smiled. So long as he had his freedom, that was all that mattered.

"But he's not happy."

My breath caught in my throat. "What do you mean?"

I heard footsteps coming up the stairs. A strange couple appeared in my bedroom doorway. The man was tall and slender, his blue eyes full of care and warmth. The woman, I presumed his wife, was quite short and plump, a big cheery smile on her face.

"Hi," she said. "I'm Wendy George and this is my husband, Nick. Can we come in?"

I nodded. "Sure."

"We're Blue's owners," Wendy said, rushing to my bedside. She grabbed hold of my right hand and squeezed it tight. "We can't thank you enough for what you did for our boy. He's a challenging chap at the best of times."

Nick stood behind his wife with his hands on her shoulders. "Blue's mother died giving birth to him. The foster mare we put him with took to him initially, then two days later almost killed him when she rejected him. We were too busy to hand rear him ourselves, so we entrusted him to some friends of ours. He became rather difficult in his behaviour as he grew up and as soon as he didn't need bottle feeding, they turned him out into a fifty-acre field and let him run free as a wild horse."

I didn't know what to say. I thought all this time that Blue's issues stemmed from the mistreatment at the farm. My heart bled for him and I wanted nothing more than to go to him and soothe his pain in any way I could.

Wendy cleared her throat and said, "They lied to us and said they were working with him every day, said he was an absolute angel. We arranged for him to stay there until we had room for him back at the stud. It made sense if he was happy and they were happy for him to stay there. About a year ago, when he turned four, we sold one of our older stallions and decided to bring Blue home. When we went to pick him up, we found a wild horse with a hatred for humans so deep, we had to have him sedated just to get near him."

I gasped and put my hand to my chest. "But why did he hate people so much? If he'd just been left to roam free?"

Nick answered. "Unfortunately, their children found it funny to chase him with their quad bike and throw things at him. When we told them our plans to collect him, they decided to bring him in and try to tame him. They beat him without mercy. Eventually he retaliated and kicked one of them, putting them in intensive care for a week. Of course, when we got there, we knew none of this."

I couldn't hold back my tears. Poor Blue. How could people be so cruel? Despite all that, he chose to put his trust in me, he chose to be around me, he even led me across the moor like a guide dog, and let me on his back. I wanted nothing more than to hug him right now.

"It's ok," Wendy said, her own eyes welling with tears. "He's safe with us, we promise. We've added more cameras and bought two more guard dogs."

"But," Nick said. "He's not right. If I didn't know better, I'd say he's depressed. He won't eat or drink. All he does is stand at the back of his stable looking sorry for himself. The vet is at a loss with him. He's in perfect health otherwise."

My heart cracked in two. "Have you tried putting him out in the field?"

Wendy nodded. "All he does is stand at the gate waiting to come back in."

I took my hand back and threw off my quilt. "I need to see him."

"Whoa, hold on there, Missy," Marsha said.

I hadn't even noticed her standing in the doorway.

"Marsha, you don't understand—"

"The horse is depressed, I know, but you're on doctors' orders. That shoulder of yours isn't going to get any better if you don't do as your told."

"He needs me. If he's not even drinking, he could die. I'll be fine."

Wendy turned around and looked at Marsha. "I'm sorry," she said. "For dropping this on you. But we're desperate. He's had such a rough start to life and when we heard what Blue here had managed to achieve with him in just a few days, we had to give this a shot."

Marsha nodded. "I understand."

"It's only an hour away. I'll be back by teatime," I said, looking at Marsha with the best puppy dog eyes I could muster.

"Actually," Nick said. "We were thinking that

maybe we could discuss, with all parties of course, you being with us on a more long term, permanent basis."

My jaw dropped. What?

Silence fell for several seconds before Marsha said, "Let's get the horse settled first, hmmm?"

DCI Baker patted my hand and winked. "Told you it'd all work out."

CHAPTER TWENTY-SIX

A lot of details had to be worked out in regards to me living with the George's permanently but for now, I was going to see my soulmate, the only other living being who understood me and accepted me for my warts and all.

Marsha had insisted on coming with me. I don't think she fully understood the depths of the bond I shared with Blue but the fact she wanted to see it for herself meant the world to me. As much as I regretted putting her through hell for the last two weeks, I didn't regret what I'd decided to do by running away that night because if I hadn't, I'd have never met Blue and just as importantly, he'd have never met me.

DCI Baker had been right. The stud was absolutely gorgeous. Acres of rolling green fields, huge electric black gates at the entrance, a massive sandy coloured country house, it really was something out of a dream.

An American style barn and Olympic sized dressage arena sat behind the house. Excitement tingled through my veins. What an amazing place. This is exactly the kind of place I always dreamed of, somewhere that would be featured in movies or magazines and now suddenly, it was in my life.

We pulled up in front of the open barn doors. I jumped out before anyone could say anything and ran inside.

"Blue!" I said, running down the centre aisle, looking in the stables either side of me. "Blue?"

I heard shuffling from near the bottom end and picked up my pace. His familiar handsome face popped over the stable door. His brown eyes lit up and he whinnied at me so loud I had to stop and cover my ears.

When I reached his stable door, I yanked it open and threw my arms around his neck, crying into his mane. When I felt his nose nuzzling my back, I hugged him even tighter.

"Hey, boy," I said, pulling back and scratching his chest. "How are you doing?"

He touched his nose to my shoulder and then snuffled through my hair.

"I'm fine," I said, giggling at him. "You need to eat and drink or no more scratches."

He bobbed his head up and down, wandered over to his automatic drinker and took a long drink before settling into his pile of hay.

"Wow," Wendy said. "I'm speechless. I literally don't know what to say."

I smiled. "He's a very special boy."

"Clearly, you're a very special girl," she said, grabbing my hand and squeezing it. "We can't thank you enough."

"You don't need to thank me. I need to thank you. He's changed my life."

"I think you've changed his."

Marsha came and gave me a hug and said, "I think you've both changed a lot of people's lives."

I glanced back at Blue and smiled. "Yes, that's true. But so long as we don't run anymore then our lives won't change, will they?"

Tears flooded Marsha's eyes. "You've never wanted to stay and fight for anything before, have you?"

I shook my head.

"I'm glad you've found your home, Blue. Home

is where your heart is and he is clearly where your heart is."

As I glanced at the gorgeous Connemara stallion before me, I realised Marsha was right. I thought home was a place, somewhere you had to be, but actually home was a connection, something you felt with another living being. Blue was definitely my home and I knew I was his home too. Soul mates aren't just for people, they're for every living thing. Even wretched ankle biting terriers.

A NOTE FROM THE AUTHOR

I hope you enjoyed Blue's story. If you did, I would be eternally grateful if you could leave a review to let others know how much you enjoyed it. Even one sentence is fine. Thank you so much!

If you want to follow me and keep up to date with all my latest goings on, visit www. maggiejoanauthor.co.uk and sign up for my newsletter, or look me up on Facebook www.facebook.com/MaggieJoanAuthor

I love hearing from my readers and will always reply to you!

COMING SOON

Lady in Red
Red
The Showman's Daughter
Romeo and Juliette
Bel Air Stables

Printed in Great Britain
by Amazon